KNIGHTS
AND BIKES

KNIGHTS AND BIKES

Gabrielle Kent

Illustrated by Rex Crowle and Luke Newell

Based on the Knights and Bikes video game from Foam Sword Games!

sourcebooks
young readers

Published by Sourcebooks Young Readers, an imprint of Sourcebooks Kids
P.O. Box 4410, Naperville, Illinois 60567-4410
(630) 961-3900
sourcebookskids.com

Written by Gabrielle Kent
First published in the United Kingdom in 2018 by Knights Of.

Library of Congress Cataloging-in-Publication data is on file with the publisher.

Source of Production: Sheridan Books, Chelsea, Michigan, United States
Date of Production: July 2021
Run Number: 5022256

Printed and bound in the United States of America.
SB 10 9 8 7 6 5 4 3 2 1

For Ashoka.

May your life be a joyous quest filled with excitement, adventure, and valiant companions.

Map of Penfurzy

THE SCRAPYARD

AVALON'S PEAK CARAVAN PARK

THE GOLF COU

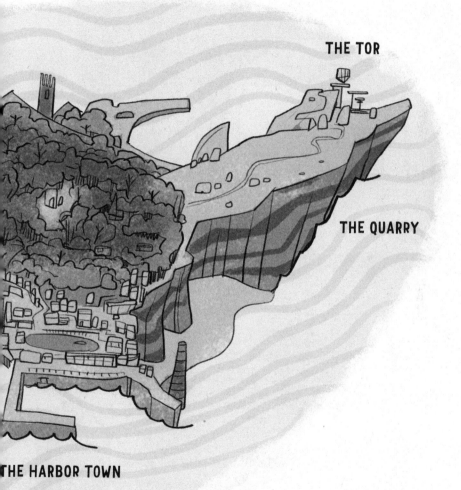

THE TOR

THE QUARRY

THE HARBOR TOWN

Chapter One
WELCOME TO PENFURZY

THE WIND HOWLED AROUND THE CABIN LIKE A
RABID BEAST AS THE RAIN CRASHED AGAINST
THE WINDOWS. THE OCCUPANTS HUDDLED
TOGETHER IN TERROR AS A SHADOWY FIGURE
LOOMED AT THE WINDOW, MOONLIGHT GLINTING
OFF THE BLADE IN ITS GNARLED HAND...

"HONNNK!"

Demelza's flashlight and the comic she was
reading were torn from her hands as her pet goose
flapped his wings furiously, causing their blanket
tent to collapse around them on the bed.

"What is it, Captain Honkers?" whispered Demelza, grabbing the goose and hugging him so close that his feathery cheek was squished up against her pale, freckled face. "Are we in danger?"

She popped her head up from the crumpled pile of blankets and peered around the little camper where they lived. Outside, the wind howled around the camper like a rabid beast as the rain crashed against the windows. Demelza and Captain Honkers huddled together in terror as a shadowy figure loomed at the window...

Demelza let out a little squeak and dived back under the blankets as the shadow slithered toward the door. "Shh, Honkers!" she hissed, shining her flashlight at the goose and clamping his beak shut between her thumb and forefinger before he could honk again. She peeked out from under the blanket. Whatever was out there had reached the door.

The handle rattled.

Demelza breathed a small sigh as she remembered locking the door before going to bed. Her relief was short-lived. A metallic scratching sound came from the lock.

"It's trying to break in!" she squeaked at Captain Honkers.

The goose flapped his wings angrily, bursting to honk.

The lock clicked again.

Demelza took a deep breath. "If we're going to be eaten by a carnivorous beast with three mouths and...and tentacles for arms, then we're going to go down fighting. Aren't we, Honkers?"

She snatched up a blanket, grabbed her foam sword from under her wooden bed, and hid behind the door. Holding up two corners of the blanket, Demelza peered over the top and watched as the door finally creaked open.

The monster slipped inside.

"Yaaaaargh!" screamed Demelza, throwing the blanket up and over the beast.

"Honnnk!" squawked Captain Honkers, pecking furiously at the thrashing creature under the blanket.

Demelza began to whack at what she thought was its head. "Die, creature of the night!" she yelled as the foam sword flailed. "Begone! Back to the pit from whence you came!"

"Mkay! Kay! Ry smurunder," burbled the creature.

Demelza stopped whacking. "Did you hear that, Honkers?" she said, wide-eyed. "It's trying to communicate." She pointed her flashlight at the struggling blanket and prodded it with her sword. "What did you say, foul beast?"

The creature wriggled away from her and struggled to its feet before flinging off the blanket and putting its hands up in the air. A large duffel bag containing something big and rectangular fell to the floor.

"I said, 'Okay, I surrender!'" said the demon, which Demelza had to admit was starting to look much less like hell-spawn and more like a girl not much older than her.

She had brown skin and punky, black hair. Her leather gloves were fingerless, and she was wearing slouchy, leather ankle boots and not one but TWO earrings in one ear. She was the coolest-looking burglar Demelza had ever seen. She was also the first burglar Demelza had ever seen.

The girl bent down to pick up her duffel bag and Demelza pointed her battered sword warily at her.

"You're not from here," she said, narrowing her eyes. "I know everyone on Penfurzy Island, and you're not anyone I know."

"Just passing through," said the girl, brushing the tip of the sword away, then rolling up her sleeve to rub at the little red peck marks Captain Honkers had left on her arm. "I thought this place was empty. I'm not sticking around—I was just looking for somewhere to sleep tonight. Sorry I scared you. I'll be going now, okay?"

"Scared?" said Demelza, her frizzy, red bunches bouncing as she leapt to block the girl's path to the door. "We weren't scared, was we, Honkers?" She grabbed the goose and held him under one arm.

"Honk!" said Captain Honkers.

"Sure. Okay, kid, you weren't scared. Now, if you'll move, I'll go and find somewhere else for the night."

Demelza stood firm. "Who you calling kid? What are you? Ten or eleven? You's just a kid, too. So, shut up, stupidhead!"

"Say it, don't spray it," said the girl, wiping her face with the back of her hand in an exaggerated motion.

"So, are you going to get out of my way? Or are you going to try to stab me to death with your toy sword?"

Demelza scratched her chin, accidentally picking the top off a scab she had forgotten was there. "I haven't decided yet," she said.

"If I do let you out, where'll you go?"

The girl shrugged and slung her bag over her shoulder. "What's it to you, short stuff?"

The wind whistled around the camper, blowing open the door and driving the icy rain forcefully against the windows. Demelza could see goose bumps all over the girl's arms. Her hair and jeans were also dripping wet, and she was only wearing a T-shirt under her light denim jacket.

Demelza chewed her lip. Even though this very strange stranger had invaded their fortress, suggested that she was scared, AND called her short, she didn't want to turn her away. She wouldn't send even her worst enemy out near the cliffs on a stormy night like this. It was a night just like this when her own mother had—

Demelza shivered at the thought and made a decision. She

slammed the flapping door shut, locked it, and pretended to swallow the key. "You're not going nowhere. Not tonight," she said firmly, then picked up her blanket and held it out to the girl. "Honkers says you can stay here with me an' him. He can sleep in my bed with me, and you can use the top bunk."

The girl pushed her wet hair out of her eyes and shrugged as though she'd be just as happy going back out in the rain, but Demelza could see a look of relief under the façade.

"Yeah, I guess I could chill here for a few hours," the girl said. "Long as you keep that Honkers on your side of the room, in case he tries to murder me in the middle of the night."

"That's Captain Honkers to you," said Demelza, putting the goose down on her bed and wrapping him up in a blanket. "He only lets me call him Honkers."

She finished tucking the goose in, kissed him on the top of his head, and turned to give the girl a sharp stare.

"Besides, as far as we know, you could be the type that does murdering—sneaking around at night, breaking into people's bedrooms. The only way to know that you won't do a murder on us in our sleep is if we're friends." She wiped her hand on her faded pajama bottoms and held it out. "You've got to know someone's name, if you're going to be friends. I'm Demelza. Demelza Penrose. I'm nine and five months. I like comics, drawing, riding my bike, and playing computer games. My favorite food is banana and peanut butter sandwiches, and I have a scar on my right knee from when Connan Lenteglos, the most annoying boy at school, dared me to do a one-eighty bunny hop on my bike. I totally did it, though!" she said proudly. "Right. Now it's your turn."

The girl paused for a minute, looking at Demelza's outstretched hand. Demelza wiggled her fingers and gave her biggest and friendliest grin, the one that showed all her teeth.

The girl finally took Demelza's hand with half a smile. "I'm Nessa," she said.

"Just...Nessa?" said Demelza. "One name. That's it?"

"Yeah. You know, like Prince."

Demelza scrunched her forehead. "Prince who?"

"It doesn't matter," grinned Nessa, making Demelza feel she was missing out on a joke.

"Well, then. Pleased to meet you, O mysterious Nessa," said Demelza, shaking her hand firmly. "The captain and I officially welcome you to Penfurzy, the bestest island in the whole wide world!"

"Honk!" said Captain Honkers.

"You're right, Honkers. She does look hungry. Nessa, we shall throw a feast in your honor!"

Demelza whizzed around her camper, opening cupboards and drawers and pulling out bags of chips, cookies, cheese, crackers, and a box of grapes. She threw them all into the center of her lower bunk and tucked a ThunderCats sleeping bag into the side of the top bunk so that it hung down to create a tent.

"Hop in!" she said to Nessa, scrambling onto the bed. Nessa slid her bag under the bed and hopped up next to Demelza.

As Captain Honkers laid his head on her knee, Demelza switched on her flashlight, lighting their faces from underneath in a manner that she thought was very dramatic. Then she tore open the packet of crackers.

"Ooh, and don't forget the guest-of-honor hat!" She pulled a battered cardboard crown out from under her bed and plonked it on Nessa's head.

"Honk!" said Captain Honkers sleepily.

"He said it suits you," Demelza said.

"Mmph, thanks," Nessa said, shoveling crackers into her mouth and biting off a chunk of Yarg cheese without even peeling off the boiled nettle leaves it was wrapped in.

"Wow, you're really hungry!" said Demelza, leaning forward, her head on her hands. "Where are you from? How did you get here? How long are you staying? And, um, why are you here?"

"Nowhere in particular. By stowing away on the last ferry. Not long; I'm just passing through. And, um, none of your beeswax."

"Ooh, you're such an iguana!"

Nessa stared at her blankly.

Demelza scratched her head. "Um, I mean an enigma."

"Yeah, that's my spy name," said Nessa. "Ann E. Nigma."

"You're a spy?" asked Demelza. Her intruder was becoming more and more interesting. "Who are you spying on?"

"I'm on a recon mission. I could tell you about it, but then I really would have to do a murder on you." Nessa grinned.

Then her mouth dropped open as she spotted something under Demelza's pillow. "Whoa, is that...? No, it couldn't be!"

She reached over and pulled out a large white and gray glove. There were plastic joypad buttons on the back of the hand and wires sticking out of the sides.

"It is!" she said in awe. "A Game Gauntlet. I've never seen a real one. I thought they were banned after they kept setting stuff on fire and electrocuting people."

"They were," said Demelza as Nessa handed it to her.

Demelza pulled on the glove and pressed some of the buttons. "It doesn't work anymore, but it was a birthday present from my mom. So I didn't return it when they were all recalled. I like to wear it for a little bit every day. You probably think that sounds silly." She blinked up at Nessa.

"I think it's pretty rad." Nessa punched her lightly on the upper arm. "Just like the kid wearing it."

Demelza felt a warm glow inside, despite being called a kid. No one had ever called her rad before.

"Honkers thinks you're rad, too," she said to Nessa. "I know you said you're not sticking around, but you're welcome to stay with us as long as you like."

Nessa's face lit up, but she chewed her nail for a while before saying anything. "You won't tell anyone where I'm staying?" she said at last.

"Cross my heart and hope to die," said Demelza, drawing an X across her chest with her finger. "Stick a needle in my eye."

"I'm afraid I'll need an even stronger promise than that," said Nessa, her face deadly serious. "There are people on this island who can't find out that I'm here." She spat in the palm of her hand and held it out.

Demelza stared at the little puddle of spit in her palm, wondering what she was supposed to do with it.

"Spit sisters," said Nessa, offering her hand again. "You know, like blood brothers but less stupid."

Demelza smiled as she understood. She spat in her own hand and slapped it into Nessa's for a very squelchy handshake.

"Spit sisters!" she said proudly as cold saliva dribbled down her arm, cementing their bond.

Chapter Two
THE PENFURZY KNIGHTS

"Wake up, sleepyhead! Don't forget to make the bed!" sang Demelza, clambering up the bed frame and resting her chin on the edge of the top bunk. She prodded the snoring lump of blankets in the middle of the mattress.

No response.

Demelza prodded again. And again.

Nessa groaned and rolled over, pulling the blankets up further over her head.

"Pancakes! I have paaaaancakes." Demelza waved a plate over Nessa's head. "Delicious, tasty pancakes! Dad made plenty, so I brought some back from the house for you."

The blanket slid down, and one of Nessa's eyes flicked open. "You told him about me?"

"No. I just told him I was extra, super hungry, so he made lots," beamed Demelza. "You're my secret," she whispered. "Spit sisters, remember?"

"Good. Let's keep it that way." Nessa's head disappeared back under the covers. A second later, her hand shot out, grabbed two pancakes, and whisked them away under the blankets.

Demelza smiled and climbed down the ladder as the sound of muffled chewing came from the top bunk. When the munching stopped and Nessa started to snore again, Demelza sat down at her desk, pulled out her pencils and paper, and began to draw. Sticking her tongue out of the side of her mouth to help her concentrate, she carefully documented her meeting with a monster who broke into her camper and turned into a girl who became her bestest friend in the whole wide world.

"Hey, you're pretty good."

Demelza jumped. She had been so wrapped up in her drawing that she hadn't even heard Nessa get up.

"I hope that's not supposed to be me, though."

"Um, no," said Demelza, sliding her pens and comic into her desk drawer and locking it shut before Nessa could reach for the page and read the story. "That's a completely different monster I had to fight last week."

She watched as Nessa looked around the camper in the daylight. Her new friend poked the origami mobile hanging from the ceiling and took in the dinosaur and space posters on the walls, the shelves stuffed with toy figures and comics, and the little record player in the corner.

"This place is great," Nessa said as she sat down and began to flick through a box of records.

Demelza blushed, suddenly unable to think of anything to say. It was strange having someone else in her camper. She didn't have many friends at school, and none of them had ever come over to visit. She knew they thought she was weird for not liking the things they liked—dolls, ballet, stories about princesses, magazines that had posters of boy bands in the middle. She bet Nessa didn't like any of those things, either.

Sidling up to the shelves behind Nessa, Demelza quickly knocked a fluffy purple teddy with a big pink heart on its chest down onto the floor. "Sorrrrrrry, Mrs. Fizziwig!" she whispered out of the corner of her mouth before kicking the teddy bear under the bed.

"Urgh, Pontefract! Total Dad music," said Nessa, pulling out a record featuring a wizard playing a steel guitar on the cover.

"Heh, yeah," said Demelza, rubbing her nose. "My dad was their roadie. He used to tour with them, until he met Mom. Pontefract paid her to make a giant lobster for one of their shows. She was an artist."

Nessa raised an eyebrow. "That's pretty cool."

"Heh, yeah," Demelza said again, looking down at her feet and hoping that Nessa would stop looking through the records before she found Jigs and Whirls for Little Girls. "What about your parents?" she asked Nessa, wondering why her new friend was out on Penfurzy on her own. "Where are they?"

Nessa shrugged. "I'm an orphan. Right now, I'm a nomad. A wanderer. Penfurzy today—tomorrow, who knows? Maybe Peru. How come you live in this camper on your own, not in the house I passed out there?"

"I just kept asking Dad until he finally let me," said Demelza, putting on her Game Gauntlet and fiddling with the buttons. "He doesn't mind too much, as long as I keep the door locked at night, eat my meals with him in the kitchen, keep the camper close to the house, and don't go wandering anywhere without telling him first."

"I'm surprised your mom is okay with that," said Nessa. "She must be pretty laid back."

"Yeah. She was." Demelza stared very hard at the dirt under her fingernails and swallowed loudly.

"Oh, dude, I'm sorry," said Nessa, getting to her feet. She picked up her bag. "Me and my big mouth. Look, I'll just get out of your hair, okay?"

"No, don't go yet!" said Demelza, suddenly afraid that the most interesting and mysterious person she had ever met was about to walk out of her life as quickly as she had broken into it. "At least let me show you around first."

"No need. I'm not sticking around. No point in getting to know the place."

"Oh. Okay, then," said Demelza, avoiding eye contact as she sat down and beckoned to Captain Honkers, who had just waddled up the steps into the camper. "It's just that Honkers wanted to show you the mini golf course that I helped build. But, you know, it's fine if you've got somewhere else to be." Demelza pulled a cracker out of her pocket, crumbled it on the rug, and pretended to be engrossed in watching Captain Honkers peck up the pieces.

Nessa scratched the back of her neck. "Well, y'know, I guess I'm in no rush…"

"Great!" Demelza leapt to her feet before Nessa could say anything further. She tucked her foam sword into her belt and swung her oversized blue windbreaker around her shoulders, tying it at the neck like a cape. "Chop-chop, then. Let's go! There's so much to see! No time to lose! The early bird catches the worm!" Pushing Nessa ahead of her, Demelza sprang out of the camper and onto the wet grass. She threw her arms wide. "Smell that clean Penfurzy air!" she cried, breathing in two lungfuls.

Nessa wrinkled her nose. "More like dirty Penfurzy butt!"

"Follow me!" shouted Demelza, grabbing her by the wrist and racing through the field, her jacket fluttering behind her as Captain Honkers waddled after them.

The golf course was one of Demelza's favorite things in the world. She was delighted to see Nessa nod her head in approval as she flipped a switch and a field full of rather rickety-looking

painted wooden sculptures came to life, wobbling and creaking and flashing as recorded voices and sound effects rang out from each one.

"Sweet! This looks totally dangerous," said Nessa, admiring a creaky, wooden ship rocking on cut-out wooden waves. It was full of grim-looking knights. "What's with all the knights and castles? Is it telling some kind of story?"

"You don't know?" gasped Demelza. "It's only the bestest story your ears have never heard. The story of the Penfurzy knights, their long-lost treasure, and the terrible curse that killed them all dead!" She pulled a battered leaflet from her pocket and handed it dramatically to Nessa.

"Two-for-one cream sodas and vouchers for half-price fishing trips and ten percent off at Saffron Records?" Nessa read out loud, wrinkling her forehead.

"Turn it over, silly!" said Demelza. "There, that's the map of our golf course with the tale of the knights that Mom wrote." She stabbed her finger onto the map, then pointed to the wooden ship they were standing next to. "This is hole number one, showing the brave knights sailing out to fight in the Crusades and to rid the world of dragons and stuff."

"Okay, so killing people who didn't believe the same as them and wiping out endangered creatures. Got it," said Nessa.

Demelza stared at her, enthusiasm wavering briefly.

"Sorry, go on."

"Well, on their journey, the knights found lots of treasure and searched for somewhere to hide it. Look, this is them in North Africa." Demelza ran to the third hole. "Here they are in

a great city in the desert, and"—she skipped over to the fourth—
"this is them finally landing on Penfurzy and deciding that this
was the perfect hiding place."

"I'm not surprised," said Nessa, rushing after Demelza. "I'd
want to hide it, too, in case the people I stole it from wanted it back."

"Oh, I don't think they stole it," said Demelza, wondering
where the knights actually had found the treasure—the legend
was a bit fuzzy on that point. "They probably just found it."

"If you say so," said Nessa.

"I do," said Demelza, although she was starting to wonder if
the Penfurzy knights were as noble as she had always assumed.
"Anyway, the knights built a BIG castle to protect the treasure, but
then they started to disappear, or suffered mysterious accidents."
She cranked a handle and a knight fell from the top of a castle
turret. Winding the handle the other way, Demelza made the
metal arm the knight was mounted on pull him back up. "The
knights who were left decided that the treasure was cursed. They
wanted to return it, but, one night, the whole castle just disappeared without a trace. No one knew what happened to it, or to the
knights or their piles of treasure. I reckon they all fought each other
to little pieces, then they rotted and their eyes fell out, and now

their skellingtons guard the treasure from anyone who comes looking for it."

"Fun story," said Nessa without looking up from the map. "So, um, did anyone ever search for the castle and the treasure?"

"Lots of people! Mainly visitors to the island. The people who live here know better. They don't want the curse to get them, too."

"So, you've never looked for it?" asked Nessa. "If I lived here it would probably be the only interesting thing I could think of to do."

"Only interesting thing?" said Demelza. "Penfurzy is full of interesting things! There's the beaches, the fun park, the arcade, the caves, the scrapyard, the quarry, the—"

"What's that, over there?" asked Nessa, wandering over to a tiny rickety shack over by the little fence that ran along the cliff edge.

"It's nothing! Don't go there!" shouted Demelza, hurrying after her. Her chest felt tight as Nessa opened the little door and crawled inside. "Get out! That's private!" shouted Demelza, her eyes prickling.

All was quiet inside. Demelza rubbed her nose, sighed, and crawled in after Nessa.

There was barely enough room for the two of them inside the shack. Demelza had to shuffle past Nessa so that neither of them ended up sitting on the other's knee. Nessa was looking around at the photos and sketches pinned to the walls. They were of a smiling woman with long, wavy red hair and freckles just like Demelza's.

"What is this place?" asked Nessa, running her finger over a painting of the sea stacks just off the shore, four pillars of stone rising from the sea just a few feet away from the cliff edge.

"It's where I come to remember Mom," said Demelza, keeping her back to Nessa so that her new friend couldn't see her face.

Nessa prodded a mobile made up of papier-mâché sea creatures, which bounced around their ears as it swung from the low ceiling.

"Just stop touching everything! You'll mess it all up. This

was Mom's stuff. I told you she was an artist. She painted all the golf course displays. Well, I helped." Demelza rubbed her nose again in the silence that followed.

Nessa touched her shoulder. "She was a very good artist."

"She was, wasn't she?" said Demelza, gazing proudly at the sculptures and paintings that filled the little shrine.

"What, um..." Nessa paused.

"Happened to her? She"—Demelza swallowed the lump that came up into her throat—"fell. Right there near the sea stacks in that painting. Dad said she'd been talking about doing something that would make everyone want to visit our golf course. He thinks she was building an extension to the course on the cliff edge when she fell."

"Sorry, D," said Nessa, putting her hand on her shoulder again. "That must have been aw—"

"Careful!" cried Demelza.

Nessa's elbow had knocked a sparkly papier-mâché lobster to the floor. They both reached for it, but it slipped through Demelza's fingers as they struggled to turn in the narrow space.

"No! You broke it!" Demelza shouted as it hit the floor and fell apart. "That was my favorite."

"Sorry! I didn't mean to," cried Nessa, grabbing the lobster and trying to fit its shell back on. She paused, removed the shell again, and looked inside.

"Why are you breaking it again?" wailed Demelza. "Give it back!"

"It's okay," said Nessa, pushing the lobster into Demelza's hands. "It's not broken. I think it's meant to open. There's something inside. Take a look."

Demelza hugged the lobster close as she reached in and pulled out a notebook. On the cover, in curly handwriting she recognized as her mom's, were the words *The Treasure of the*

Penfurzy Knights. She was vaguely aware of Captain Honkers flapping and honking outside as she began to flick through it. It was filled with notes, little maps, and sketches of an amulet, a staff, and even Penfurzy Castle!

Her heart leapt.

"Nessa, look at this," she said, thrusting the book under her nose. "Mom must have been looking for the treasure!"

They were interrupted by Captain Honkers sticking his head into the shack.

"HONNNK!"

"Whoa, chill out, little dude," said Nessa, shuffling back against the wall as the goose hissed and honked at them.

"He's trying to tell us something," said Demelza. "What's up, boy?" She squeezed out of the shack in time to see him stretch out his neck and race off across the golf course, wings raised.

"What is it, Captain?" yelled Demelza. She turned to Nessa. "Come on. Someone must be in trouble!"

She raced after Captain Honkers. He was heading toward a rumbling noise, which was growing louder and louder. She finally caught up with the goose when he stopped to hiss and shake his wings angrily at the bushes between the golf course and the camper park.

"Whazzit?" Nessa panted as she stopped next to them.

"Something...BIG," said Demelza.

The rumble became a roar. Demelza and Nessa grabbed at each other as the hedge began to shake. Suddenly, with a great tearing sound, like the splitting of the world's biggest pair of trousers, the bushes were ripped from the ground by giant metal jaws, sending mud, stones, and leaves showering down over girls and goose.

"MONSTER!" yelled Demelza.

"HONNNK!" honked Captain Honkers.

"RUUUUUUN!" shouted Nessa.

And they ran.

Chapter Three
THE METAL MONSTER

And they ran, and they ran. It wasn't until they were halfway back to the camper that Demelza realized they weren't actually being chased. She stopped running and glanced back to see what it was they were running from.

The monster was chewing up great mouthfuls of grass and soil and spitting it out in a big heap. It was also starting to look a bit less like a monster and more like a great big dirty digger vehicle. It was being driven by a skinny man with a yellow-stained mustache and a cigarette hanging from his bottom lip.

"NO!" yelled Demelza, throwing her head back and waving her fists in the air. "No-no-no-no-NO! Nessa, Honkers, stop running away!"

"What is it doing?" asked Nessa as she hurried back to join her.

"Digging up our land! That's what it's doing," growled Demelza. "The beast must be stopped! To arms!" She pulled the bent foam sword from her belt and pointed it at the digger, straightening the point as it drooped toward the ground.

"Chaaaaaaarrrrge!" she yelled, her legs almost a blur as she ran as fast as they would carry her.

"Charge!" shouted Nessa from behind.

"HOOONNNK!" honked Honkers, flapping above their heads.

The digger threw another bush on the heap and was lowering its jaw for its next mouthful of dirt when Demelza reached it. With barely a thought, she leapt into its gaping maw and pointed her sword at the man inside the cabin. The cigarette fell out of his mouth as it dropped open. He jumped down from the cabin, patting out the sparks on his trousers.

"What's the big idea?" he shouted, stomping toward her. "Get out of there, brat!"

"No, YOU get out of here. This is my land!" Demelza shouted back at him.

"Listen kid, I'm going to give you ten seconds to get down from there, or I'm going to come and get you out!"

"Then you'll be taking us both on!" said Nessa, climbing up alongside Demelza. "And we're only going to give you five seconds to clear out of here."

"Or what?" he grinned as he rolled another cigarette.

"Or we'll vanquish you ourselves, you varlet!" said Demelza, standing as tall as she possibly could and pointing her sword at him.

"What she said!" said Nessa, hands on her hips.

The digger driver lit his cigarette and threw away the match. "All right, kids, that's enough," he said. "Ten..."

"Five..." Nessa said.

"Nine..."

"Four..." Nessa said.

"Stop that!"

"Three..." Nessa said.

"I mean it."

"Two..." Nessa said.

"Right, you little—"

"One!" Nessa said as the digger driver grabbed her by the arm.

"Get him, Honkers!" shouted Demelza, furiously whacking at the man's arm with her sword.

"HONK!" honked the goose, joining the fray by dive-bombing the man, snapping at his ears.

"Aargh! Call him off!" the man shouted as Captain Honkers swept back up into the air with a beak full of hair.

"No can do!" said Nessa.

"Yeah, so you'd better get lost before he pecks out your eyeballs and swallows them whole!" said Demelza. "Eyeballs are his favorite!"

The digger driver pulled his shirt up over his head as Captain Honkers began another approach. "Just you wait until I come back!" he shouted as he began to run. "You'll regret this!"

"I regret NOTHING!" yelled Demelza, waving her sword in triumph.

"Later, dude!" shouted Nessa, hands cupped around her mouth. She nudged Demelza and held up her hand for a high five. "You're pretty brave, you know that?"

Demelza blushed as they high-fived. "Thanks for backing me up. We showed him! Didn't we, Honkers?" She scooped up the goose and gave him a big squeeze. "He said he'll be back," she said as Honkers finally managed to flap free of her hug. "We need to make sure he can't keep digging. Nessa, can you drive?"

"Sure." Nessa shrugged. "I used to be a race car driver. Put your foot down, and away you go. Easier than riding a bike."

Demelza was impressed. "But can you drive THAT?" she asked, nodding at the digger, which was still rumbling.

"Easy-peasy, lemon squeezy," Nessa said, cracking her knuckles. "Hop on board."

Demelza clambered up into the cabin and sat on the arm of the driver's seat as Nessa settled into it and took the wheel.

"Where to?" she asked.

"Somewhere he won't ever, ever be able to find it!" Demelza said. "Like, maybe..." She looked around, then pointed down the hill. "Behind those trees. Let's go!"

There was a growl as Nessa pressed a pedal. The digger lurched slightly to the right.

"Onward!" said Demelza.

There was a jerk and a roar as Nessa tried another pedal and something that looked like a joystick. There was a grinding noise, and the giant metal jaw moved upward.

"Full steam ahead, chop-chop! Let's get this show on the road," yelled Demelza.

"Look, um...this might be a little more difficult than I thought," said Nessa, waving her hand at all the little levers and pedals. "I just need to figure out which of these makes it go forward."

Demelza looked around the cabin. "It has to be one of these," she said. "Let's just try them all!" She began pulling the levers nearest to her. "Come on, let's get this thing moving before he gets back!"

Nessa shrugged and began to stomp on the pedals as Demelza flipped every switch and lever she could reach. The metal jaw flew up and down, showering the cabin with dirt and stones. Captain Honkers honked in alarm as he flew into the cabin to escape the digger's teeth.

"Ouch!" said Demelza as a big muddy stone bounced through the window, ricocheted off her shoulder and landed on one of the pedals, sending up a shower of sparks and a puff of smoke, which seemed to flow back into the pedals. Demelza wrinkled her nose as an eggy stench filled the cabin, but she hardly had time to wonder whether it had come from her or Nessa as the engine began to let out a terrible screech. Captain Honkers tried to tuck his head into Demelza's armpit and quivered with alarm.

"Whoa, hold on!" said Nessa as the digger lurched forward and began to rumble across the grass.

"Woo!" cried Demelza. "We're off! Um...maybe we should slow down a bit, though?"

"I'm trying," said Nessa. "But I can't see where we're going with that metal bucket thing in the way."

"I'll get it!" Demelza reached past Nessa and began to waggle the joystick by her elbow.

"Wait, stop!" said Nessa as the digger turned and began to rumble uphill, gaining speed. "I need to get that stone off the pedal!"

"Sorry!" said Demelza, sliding out of the way and falling onto the gearstick. Captain Honkers had had enough! He tumbled out of the side of the cabin and flew up into the air with a loud honking. Demelza grabbed a lever to pull herself up again—and it broke off in her hand!

"Uh-oh," she said as smoke belched from the exhaust pipe in front of the window. The metal jaw was moving up and down faster and faster, and the engine began making a strange screeching roar.

Nessa finally dislodged the stone from the pedal and threw it out of the cabin, but the digger was still gaining speed.

"I can't control it!" shouted Nessa over the roar of the engine as she wrestled with the wheel.

"It's possessed!" yelled Demelza. "It's trying to drive us off the cliffs! We've got to stop it!" They began pushing and pulling every pedal, switch, and lever they could find, but some of them seemed to be stuck fast. Demelza could see the cliff edge getting closer and closer. She grabbed at the key and twisted and pulled hard.

"Umm," she said, looking at the twisted bit of metal in her hand.

"Where's the rest of that key, D?" said Nessa, turning round and looking at her hand. "WHERE'S THE REST OF THE KEY?"

"It's trying to kill us," said Demelza, grabbing Nessa's shoulder. "There's only one thing we can do!" She reached out and linked arms tightly with Nessa.

"D...what are you thinking?"

Demelza looked down at the grass whizzing past under the wheels of the digger and took a couple of deep breaths. "It'll be okay," she said, more confidently than she felt. "I think we just need to hit the ground running!"

"Nope-nope-nope!" said Nessa, but Demelza was already launching herself forward.

"Geronimo!" she yelled, leaping from the cabin and taking Nessa with her.

"Aaaaaaaarrrrrgh!" screamed Nessa.

They hit the ground and went tumbling over together before they could even attempt to run away. Demelza felt the air being knocked out of her as they rolled down the hill, a ball of flailing arms and legs. They came to a stop by a very confused-looking

Captain Honkers and raised their heads just in time to see the digger reach the top of the hill.

It crashed through the fence, teetered for a brief moment, then toppled—as if in slow motion—over the edge.

Demelza counted four whole seconds before there was a faint splooooosh and a crash from the rocks below. The digger's engine stopped, and a cloud of murky blue-green mist seemed to float up from it and into the sky.

Demelza rolled onto her back, hardly able to believe their narrow escape. A laugh began to tickle inside her chest.

"That! Was the dumbest thing I have ever..." said Nessa as Demelza's laugh finally escaped. "Seriously? You're laughing?"

Demelza could hardly believe it, either,

but the laugh got louder and louder until her cheeks ached and her sides felt as though they would burst.

Nessa stared down at her in amazement, but then the corners of her mouth started to twitch until she, too, gave in to the laughter and flopped down on her back next to Demelza. They rolled from side to side, tears of relief streaming down their faces.

"DEM-EL-ZA PEN-ROSE! *WHAT HAVE YOU DONE?*" roared a man's voice.

Demelza stopped laughing. "Uh-oh." She sat bolt upright, barely noticing the digger driver running past until he stared over the edge of the cliff and let out a high-pitched scream. "Uh-oh," she said again, as a man with a bushy mustache and little beard stormed toward them until he stood over her, arms folded over a denim jacket adorned with sewn-on music patches.

"Er. Hi, Dad," Demelza said, rubbing her nose. "Dad, meet my new friend. This is Ness..."

She looked around.

"...a."

But Nessa was gone.

Chapter Four
THE AMULET OF REVELATION

"You little brat!" screamed the digger driver, hurtling back from the cliff edge, arms waving. "You killed her! You killed Gert! I'm going to whip your—"

Demelza zipped behind her dad and held onto the back of his jacket, peeking around as the man lunged toward her, his hands out like claws.

"Ugh!" he said, as Demelza's dad's palm landed in the middle of his forehead and pushed him back.

"Lemme at her!" the man yelled.

"Nope. Can't do that, Bert."

"She needs a good talking-to,

that one," the man bellowed, still trying to push forward, but walking in place as Demelza's dad kept him at bay. "C'mere, you little idiot!"

Demelza squeaked and buried her face in her dad's jacket.

She heard the sound of flapping wings, then a squelchy thud. Demelza peeked out from under her hood to see that the man had been knocked to the ground by Captain Honkers. The goose was standing on Bert's chest, wings held out threateningly as he pressed his beak against Bert's nose and glared into his eyes.

"NOBODY talks to my daughter like that," roared Demelza's dad so loudly that Demelza was sure the ground shook.

"Ah, right. Okay, sorry, Gryffyn," said the man, trying to avoid eye contact with Honkers who was hissing menacingly. "Mighta got a bit carried away there. Look, er, d'you think you could get this goose off me?"

"Here, Honkers!" called Demelza, bending down and peering around her dad's legs. Honkers hopped down and waddled over to her, turning back for one last threatening glare at Bert, as though daring him to go after Demelza again.

Demelza scooped the goose up into her arms as Bert clambered up from the ground. All the fight seemed to have gone out of him as he rubbed the back of his trousers, smearing mud all over them. "That kid of yours still needs to be punished, and who's going to pay for what she did to Gert, eh?"

"You have insurance, don't you?" asked Demelza's dad.

"Yeah, but I doubt it covers kids driving her off a cliff!" he spat.

"Well, if the insurance won't pay, send the bill to me. All right?"

Bert scowled. "Along with the bill for my lost earnings?"

Demelza's dad sighed. "Sure."

"And what about her?" Bert nodded toward Demelza. "You'll be punishin' 'er, then?"

"That's none of your business. Now go. Before I change my mind about paying you a penny."

Demelza held tight to Honkers and scooted round to stay behind her dad as he turned to watch Bert stomp off down the hill, muttering under his breath.

"Who was that, Dad?" Demelza asked, twisting her fingers through one of her frizzy bunches.

"That, Demelza Penrose, was perhaps our only hope of saving this place. And you've just sent his digger hurtling over the edge of the cliff! What were you thinking? Playing around in that thing! You could have fallen to your death. Just like..."

Demelza looked down at her feet as her dad went quiet. She pulled the strings on her hood so that it closed in around her face. "I'm...I'm sorry, Dad," she said from her nylon cave. "I just wanted to stop it tearing up the golf course, but then it got possessed! It went totally crazy. Me an' Nessa tried to stop it, but it started growling, an' roaring, an' snarling! Then it tried to drive us off the cliff!"

"Demelza! Just...just stop! Okay? Stop these stories." Her dad rubbed the back of his head, and Demelza noticed the little bags forming under his eyes.

"But it's true," she said, hugging Captain Honkers and playing with the zipper on her hoodie with her free hand. "Nessa can tell you—she saw it too."

"And where is this Nessa now?"

Demelza shrugged as she put Honkers down, then rubbed her nose. "Um, she was here a minute ago, but she just, kind of, vanished."

Her dad sighed. He picked Demelza up and hugged her tightly. "Of course, she did."

"No, she really—" began Demelza.

"Demelza. I know we haven't spent enough time together

since you moved into that camper of yours. But that's going to change soon. We'll have lots more time to spend together when we move down to a nice little house in the town."

"What do you mean, move to town?" asked Demelza, pushing herself away from her dad's shoulder to look him in the face.

"Demelza, open your eyes. The camper park is completely empty right now. You know how we've had less and less people stay here each year? Well, that means there isn't enough money for me to keep paying the bank. If I don't pay them soon, I'll need to sell the whole place, or let the bank take it."

Demelza's heart felt as though it had jumped up into her throat and wedged itself there. "Noooo, we can't leave!" she wailed. "What about the golf course? There must be something we can do to save it!"

"That's why Bert was here with his digger. He was checking the top field for mineral deposits. He wants to buy the field and part of the golf course to mine the land. That's not likely to happen now. Since I'm probably going to have to pay him for his digger, too, it looks as though I'll have to sell the whole place. And very soon."

Demelza struggled out of her dad's arms and dropped to

her feet, balling her hands into little fists. "No!" she shouted. "No-no-no!"

"Demelza, you have to under—"

"I don't have to do nothing!" Everything began to blur together as her eyes prickled with tears. "I won't let you sell it. I'm glad we killed that digger. GLAD!"

Demelza raced away across the field, cape flapping in the wind. Captain Honkers flew above her, honking loudly as if he shared her anger.

"Demelza! Come back here!" she heard her dad shouting. When she got back to her camper, she slammed the door, locked it, and sank to the floor, hugging her legs and sobbing onto her knees. A few moments later, there was a knock on the door behind her.

"Demelza. Open up," said her dad.

"No," she said, tears and watery snot running down her face and dripping off her chin.

"We need to talk. Open the door."

"NO!" wailed Demelza. "We're not moving!"

There was a pause and she heard her dad sigh. "Demelza, come out."

"I'm staying in here. Forever!"

"Okay. We'll talk when you calm down, but this move is happening. Getting angry and locking yourself up in here isn't going to stop that. Do you hear me?"

Demelza didn't reply.

"I said, do you hear me?"

"YES!" she sobbed.

"Okay." He tapped her door gently with his fingertips. "See you at dinner."

Demelza waited until she was sure her dad had gone back to the house, then she let out a gigantic wail. She put on her Game Gauntlet, picked up her bent foam sword, and furiously attacked the bunk bed ladder with it. She slashed and whacked until little pieces of foam began to break off and fly through the air.

Soon she was left holding nothing but the handgrip. She flung it across the room and threw herself face down onto her bed. How could her dad ever think of selling their home? Especially the golf course. Didn't he remember how much time Mom had spent working on it? Didn't he care?

There was a scraping noise from the window. Demelza raised her tear-streaked face from the pillow to see Nessa clambering through it. She turned and held it open for Captain Honkers as he flapped in after her.

"Could have saved myself a good whacking last night if I'd tried the window first." Nessa grinned. "Although"—she glanced at the pieces of foam sword strewn around the room—"it looks as though I'm pretty safe from your sword now."

Demelza glared at her. "What happened to you?" she hiccuped, wiping her eyes and nose on her jumper sleeve, leaving shiny streaks like snail trails on the wool.

"I had to split. I told you, I need to stay incognito."

"But Dad thought I was fibbing about the digger, and you weren't there to back me up. I thought we were spit sisters!"

"Well, you broke your promise and told him about me. And I knew I'd better stay low when he started last-naming you."

"Last-naming?"

"Yeah, DEMELZA PENROOOOOSE!" shouted Nessa in what Demelza had to admit was a pretty good imitation of her dad. "Look, I heard what he said about moving. I'm sorry. I know this place reminds you of your mom."

"Yeah, well. Not much I can do about it, is there?" muttered Demelza. She shuffled back on her bed and leaned against the headboard. "Sorry I started to tell Dad about you," she mumbled. "I didn't mean to; it just fell out of my mouth."

"Don't sweat it," said Nessa. "It was a pretty crazy morning. But, next time..." She pulled an invisible zipper across Demelza's mouth.

Demelza nodded, then picked up the little notebook they had found inside the lobster. She unzipped her mouth and said, "At least there's this."

Nessa climbed onto the bed and shuffled up next to Demelza as she flicked through the notebook, taking in all the little sketches and maps. Captain Honkers clambered onto the bed and settled behind them, stretching his long feathery neck so that he could see the notebook over their shoulders.

Demelza's mom had loved the legend of the Penfurzy knights and their treasure, but Demelza had never realized she had been searching for the treasure herself.

"Hey, turn back a few pages," Nessa said, grabbing her shoulder. "There, stop there! Look at that thing."

Demelza stared at a little sketch of a disc with a hole in the center. It was engraved with medieval squiggles.

"The Amulet of Revelation," she read.

Nessa reached into her pocket and pulled out what looked like a ball of dirt with a hole in the center. She began to clean it with her sleeve.

"Stop it!" said Demelza. "You're getting mud all over my bed!"

"Take a look at it," said Nessa, pushing it into her hand. "It's that stone that landed on the pedal when we were trying to drive the digger. You know, just before the thing went crazy. I saw something shiny in it, so I went back to find it after you had all stopped shouting and left."

Demelza looked at the muddy disc. There was metal showing through the dirt where the digger had hit it. She felt her heart begin to beat faster as she rubbed away the mud with her Game Gauntlet. As she exposed the metal below there was a hissing noise. She nearly dropped the disc when a trickle of bluey-green mist swirled out of it.

"Ew, what was that?" said Nessa, pinching her nose as an eggy smell filled the little camper.

"I don't know, but she who smelt it dealt it," said Demelza, wafting the mist away with the notebook. Captain Honkers hissed and flapped his wings to help waft away the smell.

As the mist dissipated, Demelza held the disc up next to the picture in the book. "No way!" she said.

"Way," said Nessa, her eyes lighting up. "It's the amulet! What did your mom write about it?"

Demelza ran her finger across her mum's curly handwriting. "When mounted on the Staff of Truth, the Amulet of Revelation will reveal the entrance to

Penfurzy Castle, wherein lies the cursed treasure of the Penfurzy knights." She stopped and stared at Nessa. "I don't believe this."

"A quest!" said Nessa. "Demelza Penrose, I pledge you and the captain my service. I will help you find the treasure so that you can save your home, the camper park, and the golf course—providing you forgive me for leaving you to take the blame for the digger."

"You're already forgiven," said Demelza. "But you'll be even more forgiven if we succeed in our quest."

"Then what are we waiting for?" Nessa jumped off the bed and rolled up her jacket sleeves. "There's treasure just waiting for us to find it!"

"But, first," said Demelza, dodging Captain Honkers who was running around the camper honking in excitement, "we need to find you a steed!"

Chapter Five
PRINCESS SPARKLE AND NEON JUSTICE

"No way, José. I am not riding THAT!" said Nessa.

"It's not that bad," said Demelza, looking down at the bike she was offering to Nessa while thinking to herself: it's worse.

It had been left behind by the young daughter of a family who had stayed at the camper park a few years ago. Demelza could understand why she had left it. The frame was glittery pink with a large sticker that read "Princess Sparkle." A little white basket covered in plastic daisies was attached to the front. Pink tassels swung from the ends of the white handgrips, but, worst of all...

"It has TRAINING WHEELS!" yelled Nessa.

Demelza gave them a prod with her foot. "They'll come off, no problem. So will that basket, and there's a load of spray paint in Dad's shed. We can spray it any color you like. It'll look really AWESOME!"

"If it'll look so awesome, why don't you take it and lend me your bike?"

"Umm, I think, maybe, well, uh, no," said Demelza, hugging the wide handlebars of her shiny blue bike with the chunky tires and long, comfy seat.

"Yeah, that's what I thought," said Nessa, taking the pink bike with a sigh. "Come on, then. Let's fix it up."

Captain Honkers tipped his head to one side at the banging, clattering, drilling, and sawing coming from the shed where he always found the juiciest black beetles. Waddling closer, he heard raised, muffled voices. One of them belonged to his friend, the one with the two bunches of frizzy red feathers on either side of her head. He wondered if she had any of those tasty crackers in her pockets. As he opened his beak to shout for her, the doors flew open with a bang, and a cloud of paint fumes wafted out. Captain Honkers flapped up to the roof and honked down at the two girls emerging from the shed below.

"See, told you it would look cool," said Demelza proudly as the morning sun lit up Nessa's training-wheel-free, tassel-free, pink-free bike.

"It's not bad," said Nessa, but Demelza could see a proud smile playing at the edges of her mouth as they admired the freshly sprayed black bike with its colorful splashes of bright neon paint—almost as much neon paint as was splashed across Demelza's clothes.

Princess Sparkle was gone. The frame now bore the name **Neon Justice** in luminous orange paint.

"And for the final touch!" Demelza pulled a handful of colorful square plastic clips from her pocket. "Bread bag clips! I've been saving them. They make an awesome sound." She clipped some to the spokes of her own bike and to Nessa's. "Okay, Noble Nessa. Let us mount our steeds and seek out the wise oracle." She waved up at Captain Honkers as he peered down from his perch on the roof.

"Farewell, Captain!" she cried. "You're on guard duty at the camper. Repel all invaders!"

Nessa straddled her bike and held her fist aloft. "Onward, sister!"

Despite the cold air nipping her nose and ears, Demelza felt a warm, happy glow inside her as she and Nessa pedaled full-speed out of the camper park and down the lane that led into town. Her makeshift cape fluttered against her back as they whizzed along, dodging potholes and seeing who could pull the longest wheelie—it was Demelza, but she generously admitted that her wider tires might have helped.

"Ugh. There's that stench again," said Nessa as they took a shortcut through the park, skirting a low-hanging cloud of murky mist that seemed to be creeping across the grass.

"Afternoon, Mrs. Henwood!" Demelza called to an elderly woman in a headscarf who was sitting on a bench feeding the birds. She waved to Demelza as she threw another handful of sunflower seeds down to the sparrows pecking the ground by her feet. The mist drifted over her as she waved. Demelza glanced back to see her stiffen, then scoop up a sparrow and pop it into her mouth.

"Did she just—" said Nessa, swerving to avoid a bin as she looked back over her shoulder.

"I think she was just talking to it," said Demelza, looking away quickly. "Yep, definitely just talking to it," she convinced herself. "Nothing weird at all."

Their brakes squealed as they finally pulled to a stop outside Saffron Records in the town center.

"Are you sure she's coming?" said Nessa, breathing on her fingers and stomping her feet as they secured their bikes and stood waiting. "This oracle of yours?"

"She'll be here," said Demelza, pulling up her hood and

trying not to shiver in front of Nessa. "She's always here at three on Tuesdays, and it's only ten till."

Nessa seemed to be looking up and down the street, as though watching out for someone in particular. Demelza wondered who she was hiding from.

"We could go to the comic shop while we're waiting?" she suggested.

Nessa didn't answer. She had turned and was standing at the window of the record shop, nose and hands pressed against the glass. "Who is that?" she asked, her mouth leaving a patch of steam on the window.

Demelza joined her at the window and saw a young woman with a ghost-white face, black lipstick, and lots of dark eye makeup rearranging records in the racks.

She was wearing a ripped black T-shirt and jeans, lots of silver jewelry and an enormous pair of boots covered in buckles and chains. Nessa was staring at her as though the woman had just jumped over a double-decker bus with her bike wheels on fire.

"Oh, that's Karensa," said Demelza. She knocked on the window and waved with both hands. "HEEEY, Karensa!"

Nessa went pink.

"Hey, 'Melza. What's happening?" said Karensa, opening the door and waving them into the warm shop.

"Lots of things are happening!" said Demelza. "We rode this digger an' it came to life and tried to drive us off the cliffs, then we found—" She stopped as she felt Nessa give her a little pinch, realizing that it might not be a good idea to say anything about finding the amulet before they had their hands on the treasure.

"...we found a T. rex skellington, right where it had been digging!" finished Demelza, proud of changing the end of her sentence so convincingly.

"Cool," said Karensa, placing a record with a banana sticker on its cover into the V section.

"Cool," repeated Nessa, who suddenly looked to Demelza as

though she had forgotten how to stand properly. Or was she trying to copy the way Karensa was standing?

"You're new," Karensa said to Nessa. "Are you related to—"

"She's just passing through," Demelza said quickly, before Karensa started asking questions. "Hey, do you know anything about the Staff of Truth?"

"Yeah, they're okay. But, if you ask me, they totally sold out with their last album."

Demelza scratched her head. "I meant the Staff of Truth from the legend of the Penfurzy knights."

"Oh, that Staff of Truth," said Karensa. "When my gran told me the legend, she said that the staff fitted together with the Amulet of Seeing."

"No, no," said a woman with long, braided hair, popping her head up over the record stands.

Demelza recognized her as the owner of Apache's Tears, the crystal healing shop a few doors down. The woman hurried around to join them, her rainbow-colored cardigan trailing across the floor, a record labeled Pan Pipes of Peace under her arm.

"It's the Ring of Revelation," she whispered dramatically.

"You fit the two together and hold the staff high while standing naked on the beach at sunrise on the longest day of the year."

"Nah," said Karensa. "Gran said you fit the amulet on the staff, then take it to the highest point on the island and throw it like a javelin. Where it lands is where you dig for the entrance to the castle."

"Rubbish!" shouted a little white-haired man waving The Greatest Love Songs in the World above his head, his wrinkly face more beard than skin. "You look at the sea through the amulet and point with the staff. You'll see it glow when it points to the sunken entrance."

"It's not under the sea," said Karensa. "It's under the theme park."

"How can it be under the theme park when every-one knows the entrance is in the old quarry?" said the Pan Pipes lady.

"Okay, thank you," said Demelza, trying to end the conversation, but everyone seemed to have forgotten about her and Nessa.

"The quarry? Utter rot!" shouted the bearded love-song man. "It's under the sea near the docks. All the fishermen know that. It's why there's no fish around there. Because of the curse!"

"Ah, the curse!" murmured all three together.

The conversation turned to stories of people who had touched cursed items left by the Penfurzy knights.

"My great-great-granny dug up a coin while weeding. After she touched it, she ran and grabbed a pair of shears. Before anyone could stop her, she cut off her own nose and ate it!" said Karensa.

"When I was a boy," said love-song man, "I took a man fishing. He reeled in a golden goblet. The second he laid fingers on it, he turned into a fish and leapt into the sea, never to be seen again!"

"That's nothing," said Pan Pipes lady. "When I was sleepwalking one night, I saw a magpie pick a gold ring out of the ground. As it flew away into the sky, it turned into a shower of dust. Everywhere the dust landed, the land cried out in pain!"

"Well, just last week I—"

Demelza wrenched herself away from the bizarre conversation as a vehicle backfired outside. She grabbed Nessa by the arm and dragged her outside, as tales of victims of the curse became more and more outlandish. "Come on," she said. "She's here!"

Outside, an old-fashioned green van was rumbling down the street, bouncing out of every pothole. Its brakes whined as it pulled to a stop and it let out a long hiss as it settled into its spot in the town square.

"Hi, Elizabeth!" shouted Demelza as a woman in green tweed and rain boots jumped down from the driver's seat.

"Hello, Demelza," said the woman, tying back her long gray hair and adjusting her glasses on her nose before opening the doors at the back of the van.

"Wait—stranger danger!" Nessa called as Demelza ran to the van and hopped in.

Demelza popped her head round the door. "It's fine," she said. "Come in and see."

Nessa climbed warily into the van, and Demelza smiled to see her friend's jaw drop as she looked around.

"It's a library," said Nessa, running her fingers along the book-lined shelves.

"Only the bestest library in Penfurzy!" said Demelza, spinning around. "Well, the only library in Penfurzy. There's the history books, here are all the adventure stories, there's the videotapes, and here's my favorite shelf—the comics! I've nearly read all of them."

"Whoa, there's even Judge Doom and The XYZ Warriors!" said Nessa, rifling through the contents of the shelf.

"Speaking of comics..." said the librarian. "Demelza, when are you going to return Catastrophe on Limitless Jupiters and The Woman of Iron?" She consulted a little book. "Both overdue by six days."

"Umm, next week. Definitely," said Demelza, trying to think of where she had put them, then quickly changing the subject when she couldn't remember. "We'd like to borrow some books on the Penfurzy knights, please."

"Phftt! The Penfurzy knights," scoffed the librarian. "That legend masquerading as history? No, I only have real history books in my library. If you want to hear stories about the myth that has everyone with a metal detector digging up our island, then just ask anyone in town. They all have their own versions. I seem to remember your mom asking me about the legend a few years back, but at least that was research for the golf course, not some pipe dream of finding it. I hope you girls haven't been swept up in that nonsense?"

"Heh-heh," said Demelza, scratching the back of her neck and looking sideways to Nessa.

"As if!" said Nessa, standing up. "No, we were just listening to everyone arguing about it in the record shop and thought we'd do a project on it and how it seems to drive everyone a bit bonkers. Y'know, like the Gold Rush in the Wild West."

Demelza beamed at Nessa and nodded enthusiastically. "That's it. We wanted to research the original version of the legend before writing about it."

"Ah, two scholars in the making!" said the librarian with a

nod of approval. She pushed her glasses further up her nose and looked closer at Nessa. "I haven't seen you before. Would you like a library card?"

"I'm good, thanks," said Nessa. "I won't be sticking around. But, if you could tell us anything you might have heard about the Staff of Truth, we'd really appreciate it."

"The Staff of Truth," said the librarian with half a smile. "Well, there isn't a stick of truth in the Staff of Truth..." She paused and looked at them, one eyebrow raised.

Demelza realized that she was making a joke and laughed, too loud and too late, then felt awkward as the librarian had already started talking again.

"As I said, despite it not existing, it has always been featured strongly in the legend as part of a device that will allow the bearer to see the location of the entrance to Penfurzy Castle. Demelza, do you remember the iron sculpture of the knight that stood in the center of the town square? Hmm, you might be too young."

Demelza bit her lip and looked at the ceiling out of the corner of her eye. "I think I remember being a bit scared of it," she said. "It was very old, and the face had nearly worn off. Did it hold a spear?"

"Not a spear. That was the Staff of Truth. Not the real one, of course, seeing as it doesn't exist."

"Of course not," said Demelza.

She nudged Nessa, and they both laughed along with the librarian.

"What happened to the statue?" asked Demelza. She hadn't noticed it had gone, but realized she hadn't seen it in a few years.

"Pulled up to make way for the new market square. Madern Stibb took it to his yard. Said that, as he's the King of Scrap, he should have a knight to guard his kingdom. Thinks he's King Arthur, that one. Speaking of which, can I interest you in some real historical warriors? Perhaps this book on warrior queens Boudica, Zenobia, and Mavia, who each led armies against the Romans? Or this one on Joan of Arc, who commanded France's entire army against the English at only age seventeen...or perhaps you'd like to read about Lady Triệu

Trinh from third-century Vietnam—she rode into battle on the back of an elephant whilst wearing golden armor and carrying two swords? Or how about—"

"We'll take them all!" said Demelza, holding her library card aloft. "Stamp me up!"

"Maybe we should have just taken one or two," panted Nessa as they finally got back to the camper and unloaded the piles of books, which were strapped high on their bikes. "My legs are burning!"

"Not as much as my curiosity!" said Demelza, staggering through the camper door and dropping an armful of books onto her bed as Captain Honkers came flapping in to greet them.

"That was the cheesiest thing I've ever heard," said Nessa, giving her a shove. "So, shall we go to the scrapyard to find that statue?"

"It's going to get dark soon, and I need to go in for dinner now," said Demelza, sweeping up Captain Honkers and hugging him so tightly he let out a little squeak. "I guess I'd better apologize to Dad, too. But, first thing in the morning, we'll visit the King of Scrap and see if his knight can give us any clues to where we can find the real Staff of Truth."

Chapter Six
THE STAFF OF TRUTH

The morning sun had only just started to melt the frost that had formed overnight as Demelza and Nessa bid goodbye to Captain Honkers, who looked rather offended to be left behind again, and pedaled out of the camper park. The bread tags on their spokes whizzed around, making their bikes sound like roaring motorcycles as they lifted their legs and freewheeled down the hill. Demelza's cape fluttered out behind her as they skirted the marshes and then followed a dirt road running alongside abandoned train tracks for about ten minutes.

"Behold the mighty gates of the Kingdom of Scrap," said Demelza, slowing down as they reached a wall made of corrugated iron and old wooden panels.

They followed it until they reached a set of towering wire, mesh gates.

"Madern doesn't like kids messing around in his scrap,"

TRESPASSERS WILL BE EATEN!

BODY PARTS WILL NOT BE RETURNED!

BEWARE THE DOGS!

KEEP OUT THAT MEANS YOU!

said Demelza as Nessa stared up at the many metal warning signs covering the gate.

"Dogs?" said Nessa.

"Fierce ones! Connan Lenteglos said one of them has three heads. It nearly bit his hand right off when he went in after his football. Don't worry, though. I'm pretty sure they're only let loose at night."

"Hmm, well, if you're sure," said Nessa.

"Pretty sure." Demelza began hammering on the mesh gates with a loud, crashing noise. "Madern! Madern!"

Crash-crash-crash!

"Maaaaderrrrrrn Stibb!"

"WHAAAAT?" came a crackling roar.

The girls jumped and looked up to see a rusty speaker hanging from the top of the fence beside the gate. A security camera hung next to it, its glass eye glaring down at them.

"OH, HELLO, MR STIBB!" shouted Demelza, waving at the camera. "Can we come in and look at the old Penfurzy knight statue?"

"Bug off!" crackled the speaker. "This ain't no place for kids!"

"But my friend wants to see it."

"She can bug off, too!"

"Pleeeeeeeeeeease?" shouted Demelza. "We'll be really quick. You won't even know we're there."

The speaker remained silent.

"Never heard a king talk like that before," said Nessa. "And I've met loads of them."

Demelza pushed her nose through the mesh fence, gazing forlornly around the scrapyard for the statue. "Maybe he'll be in a better mood tomorrow. We could come back and try again in the morning."

"Why wait?" said Nessa. "We could storm his castle's walls right now." She beckoned Demelza out of the view of the camera, then took off her denim jacket and tied it around her waist. "Here, give me a boost."

Demelza felt goose bumps run up her arms as she looked around to make sure no one was watching. She cupped her hands, and, as Nessa put her booted foot into them, she heaved upward.

Nessa leapt for the top of the fence, grabbing it with one hand and using the other to throw her jacket over the rusty barbed wire at the top. Demelza held her breath as Nessa climbed up and did a little flip over the jacket, lifting her legs clear of the spiky wire. There was a crunch of gravel as she dropped down on the other side, pulling her jacket down after her.

Demelza was still holding her breath a minute later when she heard bolts slide back somewhere further along the wall. She rolled into a bush in case Madern had come out to see what they were doing.

"Psssst!"

Demelza stuck her face out through the leaves.

Nessa was leaning out of a little door set into a wooden segment of the fence. "Get over here!" she hissed.

Demelza rolled out of the bush and quickly shoved the bikes into her hiding place in case Madern came out and saw them. She ran toward Nessa, who pulled her into a little shed filled with filing cabinets and a fuzzy monitor that showed the view of the gates through the camera they had seen hanging there. "You're amazing!" she said, shaking leaves and twigs from her hair as Nessa locked the door to Madern's office behind them. "Where did you learn to do that?"

"I saved a ninja's life once," said Nessa, with a shrug. "He taught me a few things. Wanted me to join his clan, but I had to keep moving. Come on, let's go and find the statue before that Madern guy comes back from the bathroom."

Demelza followed Nessa out of the little shed via another door that led out into the scrapyard itself: a vast open space filled with towering walls of scrap—from crushed cars and iron girders to unidentifiable hunks of rusted metal.

"Whoa! I bet this is how Theseus felt in the Minotaur's maze," Nessa said as they stood in the shadow of the metal walls.

"What? I read, too!" she said as Demelza looked up at her in surprise. "Now, where do you think this knight is hiding?"

Demelza chewed one of her curls as she looked around at the teetering piles. "Hmmm...Elizabeth said that Madern took the knight to be his guard. Sooo, if he's not guarding the gate, he must be at the center of the maze, guarding the whole kingdom!"

"Good thinking, D!" said Nessa. "Now we just need to figure out where that is—and quickly."

Demelza felt dizzy as they scurried down the avenues of scrap, heads swinging from side to side as they searched for the knight whilst keeping eyes and ears open for Madern and his three-headed dogs. It was as if the stacks had rusty claws reaching out to snag their clothes as they hurried past. Demelza was glad she'd had a tetanus shot recently. She wished they had brought Captain Honkers to support their search from the air.

"Left or right?" said Nessa, leaping over a kitchen sink as they reached the end of two stacks.

"Right!" decided Demelza, dodging around a wheelbarrow full of nuts and bolts. This process went on, and on, as they traveled deeper and deeper into the heart of Scrapland.

Right at a windowless double-decker bus.

Left at an old truck, wheels in the air like an overturned beetle.

Left at a van with a peeling surfboard painted on the side.

Right at a cluster of fairground bumper cars that Nessa looked back longingly at, as if desperate to stop and try them out.

Right at a stack of bike frames that Demelza was sure were watching them sadly, longing for someone to save them and take them on adventures once again. "Sleep well, noble steeds," she whispered, spinning a wheel as they ran past.

They rounded the next corner into a clearing and saw it—encircled by an ornate Victorian bandstand frame stood a knight in armor, helmet held under one arm as he raised his spear to the sky. No, not a spear...

"The Staff of Truth!" Nessa whispered.

They stared up at the statue. The knight was covered in an orange film of rust, but there wasn't a patch of rust on the staff itself.

"It looks like a different metal than the knight. Look at that green tinge. I think it's bronze, just like the amulet. You don't think it could be..."

"The real staff!" said Demelza.

"I'll keep a lookout while you check it out," said Nessa.

Demelza took out her mom's notebook and entered the knight's enclosure, holding up the page featuring her mom's sketch of the staff next to the knight.

"Six edges," she counted, "and the Penfurzy knights' crest engraved into the bottom." She squinted up at the top of the staff to see a U shape, about the right size to hold the Amulet of Revelation.

Could the Staff of Truth really have stood in the town center for years without anyone knowing what it was?

"This is it, Nessa!" she shouted, forgetting to keep quiet. "It's the real thing!"

"Grab it, and let's get out of here, then!" Nessa called back. She jumped down from her lookout point on top of a tractor, then let out a cry of disgust. "Ugh, dog poo!"

As Nessa moonwalked back and forth, leaving streaks of dog poo on the ground, Demelza tucked the notebook into the back of her jeans, reached out her hand to take hold of the staff, and began to pull, fighting against years of rust.

It started to slide from the knight's hand with a screech that made her teeth want to jump out of her mouth.

Then it stopped. Demelza yanked again, but it wouldn't

budge. She pinched her nose as the now-familiar eggy smell that seemed to have invaded Penfurzy crept into her nostrils.

There was a metallic creak. Demelza looked up.

The Penfurzy knight's half worn–away face was looking back down at her. She hooked her finger over her chin, trying to remember if his head had always been in that position.

With his one good eye, he blinked.

"Nessa," whimpered Demelza, backing away as the knight dragged his staff back out of her grasp and began to crick his neck. "Nessaaaa!" she called a bit louder as the statue flexed his arms and legs, sending down a shower of orange rust.

"What?" said Nessa, still scraping the edge of her boot along the ground. She looked up and froze as she saw the statue stepping down from his base.

"BOOK IT!" yelled Demelza, running toward her.

Nessa booked it.

Chapter Seven
ESCAPE FROM SCRAPLAND

Demelza raced after Nessa. She didn't need to check if the statue was in pursuit. The ground was shaking under the heavy iron feet pounding the gravel behind them.

They took a left at the stack of bike frames.

CRASH! went the frames behind them as the statue swept them aside.

A single bike wheel whizzed past Demelza as they turned left at the fairground bumper cars.

SMASH!

The bumper cars were flung into the air to thud into the ground behind the statue.

"Faster, D!" Nessa yelled over her shoulder as they turned right at the van with the painted surfboard.

CRUNCH-CRUNCH-CRUNCH!

The knight pounded the van out of his way.

Demelza's lungs felt like they were going to explode as she tried to keep up with Nessa, who was disappearing farther into the distance, leaping over scrap like an Olympic hurdles champion.

Demelza skidded to turn right as she passed the overturned truck with its wheels in the air like an overturned beetle.

SKRISSSSH! The truck scraped across the ground as the knight shoved it from his path.

Demelza went right at the windowless double-decker bus, charging up yet another long avenue.

BOOM! The knight toppled the bus, sending it crashing into a wall of scrap that shuddered. Pieces of metal rained down from the stacks.

Nessa was nowhere to be seen.

"Wheelbarrow-wheelbarrow-wheelbarrow..." panted Demelza, looking frantically for the wheelbarrow full of nuts and bolts where they had turned right.

There was no wheelbarrow to be seen.

A corrugated wall loomed at the end of the avenue—a dead

end. She looked over her shoulder. The knight was stomping slowly toward her, seemingly aware that he had her trapped. Demelza looked around wildly.

There was nowhere to run.

"Halt!" Demelza shouted, picking up a shovel and waving it in front of her.

The knight didn't halt.

"Get back!" she yelled, dropping the shovel and picking up a length of chain.

The knight kept coming.

Demelza began to swing the heavy chain around her head, slowly, at first, but it picked up speed until it was whizzing through the air in a blur like a helicopter blade above her head.

THWUM-THWUM-THWUM.

Demelza lined it up with the knight's legs. "Take that!" she shouted, letting go of the chain and watching it fly, waiting for it to wrap itself around the knight's legs and topple the statue, just like she'd seen in films.

It didn't.

It missed, slithering harmlessly across the ground and wrapping around an old gas pump.

"Sorry, Mr. Knight! Uh, Sir Knight!" Demelza squeaked as she backed away from the advancing statue.

The only shelters she could see anywhere near were a large mobile home and the cabin of what looked like a tall crane. The mobile home was closest, so she ran for it, leaping through the open door and slamming it shut behind her. She scurried over to hide under the dining table in the little kitchenette, pulling the little gingham tablecloth down like a curtain. Her blood pounded in her ears as she tried to get her breath back as quietly as possible. She wondered if Nessa had gone to get help.

As she finally calmed her breathing, Demelza realized that she could no longer hear the creaking joints or pounding footsteps of the iron knight. She waited a few moments more, then slipped out from under the table.

Brushing aside one of the orange curtains covering the little grimy windows, she peered up and down the avenue. There was no sign of the knight. The coast seemed clear through the front windscreen too. Maybe the knight had gone after Nessa?

Demelza hoped her friend had managed to get clear of the scrapyard. She scurried to the back of the van for one last check through the rear window, gently lifting the curtain and peeking out.

A large iron head peeked back at her.

"Aaaaargh!" screamed Demelza, half running, half tumbling to the other end of the vehicle as the knight lifted the back end into the air and began bouncing the mobile home up and down.

Demelza dodged swinging cupboard doors and falling drawers as she dived back under the table and held onto its legs, very grateful that they were tightly bolted to the floor.

"I'm... sorry... I...tried...to...take...your...staff!" she shouted between gasps as her whole world bounced up and down. Just as she thought she couldn't hold on any longer, the bouncing stopped. Before she could take a breath, the window exploded into the room as the knight's iron fist came through it. His big metal arm waved around, knocking over everything in its path as he searched for Demelza. She managed to wriggle under one of the seats and lay there biting her knuckles.

The hand came closer, and closer, fingers feeling every surface. Demelza saw a mop lying nearby. She wriggled forward on her stomach and grabbed it, holding the shaggy end in the path of the searching fingers. The hand stopped and explored the top of the mop as if trying to work out if it was Demelza's hair, then grasped it so tight the wooden handle splintered as it was whisked out of the window.

Demelza rolled back under the seat and listened, but the knight wasn't fooled for long. The hand shot through the window again, sweeping around until its fingers were only inches from her face. She pressed herself back as far as she could get from it, but, any second now—

"Hey! Iron Man!" shouted a distant voice as rock music began to blast out of crackly speakers.

The hand stopped moving, then withdrew slowly as an engine roared and a chain began to clank. Demelza could hear the knight's footsteps pound away from the mobile home. She slid out from under the chair and looked out of the broken window. The knight stood a few feet away, staring up at the crane. The music was blaring out of the cabin, and someone was leaning out and making rude gestures at the knight.

It was Nessa!

Nessa pulled a few levers in the crane, and the arm swung around to dangle a big, round metal disc over the knight. It began flinging scrap aside as it tried to reach her. She mimed something at Demelza, waving one arm rapidly as the other controlled the crane.

"What?" shouted Demelza, struggling to make herself heard over the music and crashing debris.

The knight hurled a scooter toward the cabin of the crane.

Demelza flinched, waiting for the sound of smashing glass— but it didn't come. She opened her eyes.

The scooter hadn't reached the cabin. Something strange was happening. It boomeranged back and flew up to clang onto the metal disc. Other small pieces of metal were beginning to fly up toward it.

"Electromagnet!" gasped Demelza, suddenly understand- ing Nessa's warning as the mobile home began to shake. Running for the door as the front end began to lift into the air, Demelza jumped from the vehicle as it slid across the ground.

As she hurried away from the flying debris, she could see that the knight was trying to run, too, but he wasn't getting very far. For every step he took, he slid farther backward toward the magnet. Finally, with a metallic wail, he flew up into the air and clanged into the disc, followed by all the loose pieces of metal lying nearby. One by one, they flew up to join the flailing knight as he slowly disappeared from sight. With a huge THUNK, the back end of the mobile home thudded into the knight, covering him completely as it hung there with the front grille still touching the ground.

A murky blue-green mist spilled from the ball of metal clinging to the magnet, an eggy stench wafting out with it. Demelza jumped back as the stink cloud floated past her and away through the yard.

"You saved my life!" cried Demelza, running toward Nessa as her friend swung down from the cabin.

"Oof!" said Nessa as Demelza crashed into her, hugging her tightly around the waist. "Look out!" She flung Demelza backward as a metal pole hit the ground with a clang right where she had been standing.

"The Staff of Truth," gasped Demelza. She lifted one end of the heavy, metal staff and looked up at the magnet. "How come it didn't stick?"

"I was right. It's bronze," grinned Nessa. "Bronze isn't magnetic." They picked up the heavy staff between them.

"WHAT HAVE YOU DONE TO MY SCRAPYARD?" bellowed a voice.

"Uh-oh. Madern!" squeaked Demelza as a burly man with gray stubble and skin like leather stormed toward them. He was rolling up his sleeves, eyes blazing under a trucker cap.

"Book it!" shouted Demelza for the second time that morning.

Holding the staff between them like a battering ram, they ran as fast as they could, Demelza's feet barely touching the ground as she was pulled along by Nessa.

"Get back here!" roared Madern, reaching out to grab them as they raced past.

"He's got a bad knee; he won't chase us far," Demelza called to Nessa as Madern limped after them at full speed.

"It's not him I'm worried about," shouted Nessa. "It's them!"

A distant barking grew louder. Demelza turned her head

to see three huge German Shepherd dogs bounding along the avenue to their left, their huge paws kicking up a cloud of dust as they skidded to a halt at the end of the avenue, waiting for instructions from Madern.

"The three-headed dogs!" shouted Demelza.

As the dogs stood panting, the murky mist drifted out of one of the stacks and rolled over them, flowing into their mouths and nostrils. Their ears flattened against their heads as they bared their teeth and began to snarl. Demelza yelped and put out an extra burst of speed as the dogs shot after them, their eyes gleaming black.

Madern's shed-office came into view as they turned left at the wheelbarrow full of nuts and bolts. The staff seemed to be getting heavier, and the shed—with its door out of the Scrap Kingdom—was still so far away...

The slavering dogs quickly closed the gap.

"Rocky, Apollo, Clubber, stop, heel!" yelled Madern from a long way behind them. "What's wrong with you?"

"They're going to eat us!" yelled Demelza, her feet moving so fast that she was afraid her legs would fall off as Nessa sped her along. With only seconds to spare, they tumbled into the shed. Dropping the staff with a clang, Nessa slammed the door and held it shut while Demelza slid the bolts into place. There were three thumps as the dogs hit the other side of the door, panting and growling as they leapt up and scratched at the wood.

"That...was...close!" panted Nessa, sliding down the door until she was sitting on the floor next to Demelza as the two of them caught their breath. "Come on, let's get this thing back to your camper."

Chapter Eight
THE QUEST

"Oh, shoot," said Demelza as she cycled triumphantly up to her camper with Nessa, staff held between them. Her dad was standing at her door, arms folded across his chest as he watched them cycling up the road.

"I guess there's no point in hiding now," said Nessa. "He looks pretty mad."

Demelza could see Captain Honkers peering out from where he was cowering behind her dad's legs as though feeling guilty for not having warned them.

"Hey, Dad," said Demelza as they reached the camper and

dropped their bikes and the staff into the grass. Captain Honkers flew over to peck affectionately at her loose shoelaces.

"Don't 'Hey Dad' me." Demelza's dad looked from her to Nessa. "Who is your friend?"

"This is N—ehhhh," began Demelza, trying to think quickly.

"Cyndi!" Nessa jumped in. "Cyndi Lennox. Pleased to make your acquaintance, Mr. Penrose."

Demelza was surprised at how very formal and polite Nessa sounded as she held out her hand to shake her dad's.

He looked at Nessa, one eyebrow raised, as if unsure whether she was being cheeky, then shook her hand, chest deflating a bit.

"What have you two been doing? I've just had a call from Madern Stibb. He said you broke into his scrapyard and destroyed it."

"We couldn't help it!" said Demelza, waving her arms in the air. "A giant Penfurzy knight was chasing us. Ne—Cyndi defeated it, but then Madern set his three-headed dog on us!"

"Demelza! Again with the stories. Life isn't just one big adventure."

"Sorry, Mr. Penrose," said Nessa, stepping forward. "Demelza was giving me a tour of the island, and I really wanted to see the scrapyard. We didn't mean to cause anyone any trouble. And there were actually three dog heads, only they were on three different dogs."

Demelza saw the briefest hint of a smile pass her dad's lips.

"Well, I'm not sure how anyone could wreck a whole scrapyard. Madern hates intruders, and Demelza knows that. I'll pop over to speak to him tomorrow, and, Demelza, I expect you to give him a full apology."

"I'll make him a card and draw him a picture to show I'm reeeeeally sorry," said Demelza.

Her dad gave her an approving nod, then turned his attention to Nessa.

"I haven't seen you around before, Cyndi. Do you live here on Penfurzy?"

"No, Mr. Penrose. Just staying with a friend. I'm not sticking around."

"Ah, so you're not related to the—"

"No, sir, not related to anyone here," Nessa said quickly. "What makes you think I might be?"

Demelza thought her dad suddenly looked very awkward as he rubbed the back of his neck. "Oh, uh, no reason. Well, just make sure that neither of you gets into any more trouble this week. Demelza is a mischief magnet, and I've more than enough to worry about right now."

"Yes, Mr. Penrose. I'll look after Demelza."

"Right then." He nodded, then clapped his hands together. "You might as well pop in for lunch with us, Cyndi. Mrs. Bocaddon just brought round a freshly made stargazy pie."

"Stargazy pie?" Nessa whispered to Demelza as they followed him into the house, Honkers waddling along behind.

"You're in luck," said Demelza, swallowing all the drool pooling in her mouth. "Mrs. Bocaddon makes the best stargazy pie you'll ever eat."

Demelza was surprised that Nessa didn't look particularly excited about her first stargazy pie as they sat down at the kitchen table in front of a roaring fire.

She pushed the big round pie dish toward Nessa and poked at one of the ten pilchard heads sticking up out of the crust. "It's stargazy 'cause the fish are gazing at the stars, see?" said Demelza. "It's got fish, potato, and egg in it."

"Um, thank you, Mr. Penrose," said Nessa as Demelza's dad cut into the pie and heaped a slice onto her plate.

Two fish heads stared up out of it.

"You don't have to eat the heads, not if you don't want to," said Demelza, stabbing her fork into a fish head so hard the eyeball popped out and was promptly snapped up by Captain Honkers.

"I'm glad Demelza has made a real friend," said Demelza's dad, pushing Captain Honkers away as he tried to peck a whole pilchard out of the pie. "It can get a bit lonely up here during the school holidays. It's a shame you're not sticking around for long. But you're welcome to visit if you're ever back. Maybe your good manners will rub off on Demelza. I'm hoping she'll see a lot more of her school friends when we move down into the town."

"Don't talk about me as though I'm not here," said Demelza through a mouthful of sardines. "And what do you mean, when we move to town?"

"Demelza, let's not do this now," said her dad.

Demelza felt her temper rising. "I told you, I won't go!" she said, banging the end of her knife on the table. Nessa looked at her plate uncom-fortably, pushing a sardine around with her fork.

"Demelza, there's no

other option. We need to sell up and leave. Someone has made an offer on the camper park, and I'm signing it over to them the day after tomorrow."

"You can't!" shouted Demelza. "You don't need to! We're going to find the Penfurzy knights' treasure really soon!"

"I know your mom was fond of that story, but the treasure is a legend. There is no magic way out of every situation. I promise you you'll be happy living in town closer to people your own age."

"No!" shouted Demelza. "It's real. We'll prove it to you when we find it. Then you'll be sorry you didn't believe me!" She jumped to her feet and ran from the kitchen, Captain Honkers squawked and danced on the spot, trying to decide whether to follow her or to peck at the food she had left on her plate.

"I'll go and talk to her," she heard Nessa say to her dad as she flung open the kitchen door and ran back to her camper and slammed the door.

Knock-knock-knock.

"Go away!" Demelza shouted.

"You know I can just come in through the window again, or pick the lock, right?" said Nessa's voice. "I'm being polite and knocking."

"Polite!" said Demelza, flinging open the door. "Yes, you were very polite to Dad, even though he's selling Mom's golf course and making me move away from where she lived!"

"You're being a bit unfair to him, D," said Nessa, stepping into the camper. "He's just trying to do what's best for you. And don't you see what this means?"

"What?" said Demelza, wiping her nose on the back of her hand.

"We have a time limit! All the best adventures have time limits."

"Honk!" agreed Captain Honkers, flapping up the steps as Nessa pulled the staff up into the camper and held it by her side, like a spear.

"Demelza Penrose, we have thirty-six hours to find the treasure and save your golf course. Will you give me your word you will continue on your mother's quest with me as your paladin?"

"Despite dangers untold or hardships unnumbered?" said Demelza.

"As we boldly go where no one has gone before!" said Nessa.

Demelza smiled and thumped her arm to her chest, hand over her heart. "You have my word," she sniffed. "On with our quest!"

Chapter Nine
TROUBLE ON THE TOR

"Try a lower gear!" Demelza called back to Nessa as they cycled painfully slowly up the tor, calves and thighs burning.

Despite all of the confused accounts they had heard in Saffron Records of what to do with the staff and amulet, there was a grain of truth in all of the tales. According to Demelza's mom's diary, the staff should be taken to the highest point on the island. There it would reveal the location of the entrance to the castle. The highest place Demelza could think of was the tor looming over the quarry, so, first thing in the morning, they had set off to scale it, staff lashed to both bikes, holding them together like a tandem.

Captain Honkers had been left behind on guard again as he had a terrible habit of chasing the puffins that nested around the tor.

"There's another one of those weird stink clouds," said Nessa, as they passed a patch of mist that was swirling toward a wooden bench where two old men sat smoking pipes. "I wonder where they're all coming from?"

As the mist rolled over their feet, the two men dropped onto all fours and began growling at each other before being distracted by a squirrel which they chased up the nearest tree.

"That's Mr. Par and Mr. Lanner," Demelza said as Nessa stared back at the panting, whining men who were both pawing at the tree. "They're a bit odd," she whispered.

"No duh!" said Nessa.

Demelza struggled to push down on her pedals as the slope grew steeper.

"I give up. We're going to have to walk!" panted Nessa at last. "It'll be midnight by the time we get to the top at this rate."

"Okay, if you're tired," said Demelza, stopping and trying to look as though she wasn't gasping for breath herself. "We can leave our bikes here and walk to the top."

Leaning the bikes against the rocks, they untied the staff, picked it up between them and pushed on toward the summit. Demelza had spent lots of time exploring the quarry below for fossils. She had a particularly nice trilobite on her Shelf of Interesting Stuff, but she had never climbed to the top of the tor before and hadn't realized just how steep it was. Before long they were clambering on all fours as they hefted the staff up the slope between them.

The slope was pitted with puffin burrows and the pair had to watch where they put their hands and feet as they scaled the tor. It was difficult to keep hold of the heavy staff between them both, and they kept standing on each other, especially when they dodged the angry puffins that kept popping out of their burrows to snap at their fingers.

By the time they finally reached the flat plateau at the top, Demelza was feeling thoroughly fed up with nature.

They flopped down and rested against a huge pile of neatly stacked stones.

"Thanks!" Nessa said, gulping from a bottle of juice Demelza had pulled out of her dinosaur lunch box. "What's the story behind this place?" she asked, wiping her mouth with the back of her hand and patting the stone structure they were leaning on.

"Well, if you believe Connan Lenteglos, which, by the way, I don't," Demelza spat, "then his great-great-grandad carried all of these rocks up here on his back in one go. But Connan is a big, stupid liar. Dad said it's a cairn—a landmark—and people have been adding stones to it for hundreds of years. He and Mum climbed the tor before I was born and put a stone on it." She wiped the juice from her chin as she stared up at the stack of stones. "I wonder which one was theirs."

"So, what do we do now?" asked Nessa.

Demelza pulled out her mother's notebook. She flicked through it and ran her finger down the pages that mentioned the staff and amulet. "Mom thought there was some sort of base up here to fit the staff into," she said. "We just have to find it."

"It can't be that difficult," said Nessa, looking around the little plateau. "But it would be easier if we knew what we were looking for."

"Some sort of plinth," said Demelza, checking the notebook. "What's a plinth?"

"Like a slab. A base, I think," said Nessa. "Like the knight was standing on. You know, something like that." She pointed to the stone slab at the base of the cairn. Her face fell.

"Oh no," said Demelza. "You don't think that's it, do you? There must be a bazillion tons of stones on top of it!"

"Well, if people really have been adding to the cairn for as long as you say, then it's been hundreds of years since anyone saw what's on the slab at the bottom. And, if we want to see it ourselves, there's only one thing we can do..."

"Take it apart," said Demelza with a gulp. "Well, it's not like I could get in any more trouble this week." She rolled up her sleeves. "Let's get started."

The cairn stood over two meters tall and tapered inward toward the top. The stones at the top were much smaller than those at the bottom. By sitting on Nessa's shoulders, Demelza was able to shove the little ones to the ground. They both whooped as the stones toppled, some cascading down the hill, others over the steepest edge of the tor and down into the quarry below, clicking and clacking as they caught the rocky wall on the way down.

As the cairn decreased in height, they found the lower stones bigger and harder to push. When it got down to just under a meter high, they could no longer push away several at a time and had to start moving the stones one by one.

The plateau was soon littered with rocks. Demelza wiped the sweat from her brow with her sleeve as they worked, rolling larger and larger stones over the edge of the cliff with both hands, rather than risking them rolling down the hill and hitting anyone who might be out walking.

"Oof, that was a big one!" said Nessa as a rock dropped into the quarry with an echoing boom.

"Nearly there!" panted Demelza.

It had taken nearly two hours, but areas of the plinth could finally be seen between the rocks.

"There's something on it," said Nessa, pushing away a large stone with her feet.

"It's the Penfurzy knights' crest!" said Demelza, clapping her hands. Together, they pushed and pulled the largest rock out of the way to reveal the base of the cairn for the first time in centuries. "This has to be it. We've found it, Nessa!"

"And this hole here," said Nessa, brushing away the dirt

from the crest with her bare hands, "must be where we put the staff."

Demelza leaned over and watched as Nessa moved to scoop gravel from the six-sided hole in the center of the plinth. The second her fingers touched it, a dark mist oozed out of it and flowed into Nessa. A horrible smell filled the air. Nessa's hands curled like claws as she looked up toward Demelza, her deep brown irises darkening and spreading until both of her eyes were pools of black.

"Nessa..." said Demelza, backing away slowly. "Nessa?"

Nessa didn't seem to hear her. She snatched up the staff as though it were as light as a broom handle and fixed her blank eyes on Demelza. "GIVE ME THE AMULET," she commanded, in a voice deeper than Demelza's dad's.

"I...I think maybe that's not such a good idea," said Demelza, still backing away. "I think you might not be yourself right now, Nessa. I think it might be...the curse!"

"GIVE ME THE AMULET," Nessa repeated in the same deep, dead tone.

"Umm, I'm thinkinnnnng...no," said Demelza, holding one hand up in front of her as she rummaged in her backpack with

the other. "Maybe you'd better stop just there." She pulled out the first thing her fingers found in her bag—a Frisbee—and waved it threateningly in front of her. "Stay back, Nessa!"

Nessa kept walking, hands reaching out to take the amulet.

Demelza threw the Frisbee. It bounced off Nessa's forehead. She didn't even seem to notice. Demelza reached back into her bag and began frantically throwing more of the contents at Nessa.

A handful of novelty erasers bounced off her chest.

A tiny ugly plastic doll with crazy green hair skimmed her knee.

Three rubber bouncy balls ricocheted off her shoulder.

Two water balloons exploded on her head—still, Nessa kept coming.

The top of the tor was perilous with the stones from the destroyed cairn. Demelza slipped and slid on them as she danced away from Nessa who seemed fully under the influence of the curse.

Finally out of things to throw, Demelza threw the bag itself, then looked around for something else. All she could see were stones and she couldn't throw stones at Nessa, no matter how cursed her friend was.

"Nessa, please, stop!" Demelza begged, as she realized she was being forced toward the cliff edge. Stones dropped down behind her, clacking against the quarry walls on their long journey to the ground.

"THE AMULET," repeated Nessa, arms outstretched as Demelza teetered on the edge of the cliff, heart pounding as the sound of the stones hitting the ground echoing back up to them.

"NO!" Demelza shouted as Nessa lunged at her. She held out the hand on which she wore the Game Gauntlet, trying to keep Nessa at arm's length.

The second Nessa walked into the gauntlet, she flew backward through the air, landing on the stony ground with a thud. Demelza sprang away from the cliff edge and crept cautiously over to Nessa. There was a quiet hiss, like air rushing out of a beach ball, as the foul-smelling mist drifted from Nessa's mouth and ears.

"Nessa?" whispered Demelza.

There was no response. Demelza hoisted up the Staff of Truth with a grunt and poked Nessa's stomach with the end of it.

"Grruuunnnghh." Nessa opened her eyes and blinked as though she'd been asleep for hours. She sat up and rubbed her grazed elbows. "What happened?"

"You went bonkers is what happened! You was after the amulet and tried to push me off the edge of the cliff. Then my Game Gauntlet touched you, and you went flying. Then smoky stuff poured out your ears! I think it got you when you touched the plinth, cuz it was put there by the knights."

"What got me?" said Nessa, looking around groggily.

"I think it was the curse!" said Demelza. "I bet that's what made the digger and the statue go loopy too. Remember the stink when the digger threw up the amulet? Then again when we cleaned it with my glove? I thought it came from you, so I didn't say anything, but, when I touched the Staff of Truth for the first time, I smelt it and saw the mist again. It came out of the knight when you magnetificated it and drove Madern's dogs crazy. The same stinky mist came from the plinth when you touched it and came out of your ears after my glove touched you..."

"Urgh," said Nessa. "I could feel it inside me. It was like I was being moved with a remote control. It wanted to stop us finding the treasure. I'm sorry, D. I should have fought it harder."

"You couldn't help it," said Demelza, giving a one-shouldered shrug as she reached down to help Nessa up with her gloved hand. "At least you didn't chop your nose off and eat it, like Karensa's granny."

"That glove..." said Nessa, keeping hold of Demelza's hand and turning it over, examining the gauntlet's buttons and the wires looping in and out of it. "There's something special about it. I think it can break the curse."

"You mean my gauntlet blasted the curse out of you?" said

Demelza. "I knew there was something special about it. That's why I never sent it back after the other ones were recalled."

"Just as well. I have a feeling we'll need it again before our quest ends," said Nessa. "There's something funny going on on this island. Those guys down the hill, that woman in the park yesterday, maybe this curse is spreading." She pointed at the staff. "Come on, before anything else happens, let's find out where this castle has been hiding all these years. You'd better do it—and keep that gauntlet on!"

Demelza took the amulet from her pocket and placed it into the top of the staff using the gauntlet. There was a spark the second she fixed them together, then a little burst of dark mist.

"The curse again." said Nessa. "Careful!"

Between them, they hefted the staff onto the plinth and placed the end into the six-sided hole, whooping with excitement when it slotted into place perfectly. Demelza clambered onto the pile of stones, which was all that remained of the cairn, and looked through the amulet.

"What do you see?" asked Nessa.

"The horizon," said Demelza. "I doubt it's hidden way out there. What about your side?"

Demelza stepped aside as Nessa looked through the other side of the amulet.

"I can see the weather vane at the top of the town hall. That can't be right, either. I think we need to turn the staff."

Demelza lifted the staff out of the hole.

"Six sides, so that means there are six different views through the amulet," said Nessa.

Demelza turned the staff to the next position and placed it back into the plinth.

Again, they just saw boats far out at sea through one side of the amulet and the distant mainland through the other.

"You don't think it really is way out

117

there under the sea, do you?" asked Nessa as Demelza lifted the staff out of the hole and turned it to the last position.

"I heard that the castle was only ever cut off from land at high tide," said Demelza. "So it must be near to the shore. I hope so, anyway. I don't know anyone who could lend us a submarine. Unless you're a submarine captain as well as a ninja?" she added, casting a suspicious glance at Nessa.

"Nope. I was on the crew of a pirate ship for a few months, but the Barnacled Beast sank last year, so they can't help us now."

"Hmm, convenient," said Demelza, starting to wonder if Nessa's pants might be on fire. She looked through the hole. "The mainland again." She stepped back up onto the rocks at the other side of the staff to peer at the last possible location where the castle could be. Then she froze as she realized what she was looking at.

"What can you see?" asked Nessa, pulling at her sleeve. "Is that it? Do you know where it is?"

Demelza nodded as she stepped down shakily.

Nessa jumped up behind her and looked through the amulet. She gasped. "It's one of the sea stacks just off the cliff by your golf course!" Nessa's face fell. "Wait, isn't that where your mom...?" Her voice trailed off.

Demelza nodded and sat down hard, blinking rapidly. "You know what this means?" she said. "If that's where the castle is, then Mom must have figured it out." Her heart pounded against her ribs and she felt a little sick as so many thoughts flew around inside her head. "When she fell, she wasn't working on the golf course like everyone thought. She was trying to reach the stack, Nessa. Mom was trying to get to the castle!"

Chapter Ten
VANQUISHING FEAR

Demelza hardly remembered the ride home as they cycled back in silence. Her mind was whirling.

Had her mom really figured out the location of the castle, even without the staff and the amulet? What had happened the night she fell? Had she been trying to find a way to climb across to the sea stacks?

They pulled up by the cliff edge, right where Bert's digger had torn down the fence. Dropping their bikes into the long grass, they sat down, side by side, and gazed out at the four sea stacks.

Demelza had often thought it strange that they were all the same height and equally spaced, but now, sitting here staring at them, it seemed impossible that she had never seen them for what they really were. They were very weathered, covered in birds' nests, seaweed, moss, and generations of white bird poop, but there was no mistaking them now.

"Turrets," she murmured. "Castle turrets, right here, stick-

ing out of the sand where everyone can see them. All these years, and nobody ever guessed!"

"Except your mom," said Nessa, leaning in to her as they sat shoulder to shoulder. "She must have been very clever."

"She was," said Demelza.

They sat in silence for a few moments. Captain Honkers flapped over to greet them but seemed to realize this wasn't the moment for honking. He settled down next to Demelza and put his head on her knee.

"Are we still going out there?" Nessa asked.

Demelza shuddered. The turret that she had seen through the amulet wasn't actually very far away, but the rocky shore below was much farther down than she wanted to think about. She had always stayed at least a few steps back from the cliff edge since the night her mom fell, so just the thought of trying to reach the turret filled her with dread.

"We've got to," she said at last, pulling on the strings of her windbreaker. "Maybe we could go down to the beach at low tide and then climb up it?" she suggested. Before Nessa even answered, she knew it was a crazy idea. The walls were steep, and, even if they managed to scale the slimy bricks, the seabirds were likely to attack anyone climbing near their nests.

There was only one option, and they both knew it.

"We need to make some sort of bridge," said Nessa. "And, if your dad is signing over the land in the morning, it's got to be tonight."

Demelza knew she was right, but how could they get across when she couldn't even stand near the edge of that cliff? Her mom had fallen, trying to do the same thing...

"Let's go to your camper and prepare," said Nessa, seeming to sense how nervous Demelza felt. "When you go in for dinner, I'll come back out here and think about how we're going to do this. Ninja skills, remember?" she said with a grin.

They spent the afternoon carefully packing everything they thought would be of use into their pockets and backpacks: flashlights, spare batteries, rope, pocketknives, a calculator, water pistols, bubble-gum—for chewing and for gluing. Then Demelza added a toilet plunger, a small mirror—in case they came across a Gorgon (everyone knew a mirror could defeat a Gorgon)—chip sandwiches, her mom's notebook, and, of course, the curse-breaking Game Gauntlet.

Nessa packed a bag of fridge magnets, which Demelza suspected she'd acquired by letting herself into the other campers, two packets of Pop Rocks, a bag of marbles, and a couple of small bottles of cola.

Captain Honkers was very interested in all the activity and waddled around the camper honking loudly and pecking at everything they tried to put into their bags. Demelza finally had to put him outside, where he sat forlornly, watching them from the little flower box under the window.

By the time Demelza went to the house for dinner with her dad, she felt as if they were ready for anything the castle could throw at them—even if she didn't have a clue how they were going to get there.

Nessa was strapping on plastic knee and elbow pads when Demelza returned from dinner, bringing her a meat and vegetable pasty and a saffron bun.

"I've got it all figured it out," she said, spitting crumbs as she munched into the food. "You'd better get ready."

Demelza buckled on a set of pads, too, then dug around in the trunk at the bottom of her bed and pulled out a couple of laser tag breastplates. "They're busted, but they're still good for protection," she said, putting one on and passing one to Nessa. She fastened on her bike helmet, donned her Game Gauntlet, and made a fist at her reflection in the wardrobe mirror, admiring her plastic armor.

Nessa finished her food, then lay on the floor and dragged the big duffel bag she had arrived with out from under the bottom bunk.

"What is that?" asked Demelza as she watched her pull a big rectangular plastic object out of it.

"My boom box," said Nessa with a proud smile as she ran her fingers across the two cassette decks, audio sliders, and big speakers at either end. "I made us a quest mixtape." She rummaged in her pocket then held up a cassette tape.

"Hey, give that back!" she shouted as Captain Honkers snapped it out of her hand and started pulling out the shiny tape inside as though it was a very, very long worm.

Demelza pulled the goose away and watched as Nessa salvaged the cassette, inserting a pencil into one of its holes and winding the tape back into it. No one had ever made Demelza a mixtape before. She felt her excitement for the mission ahead rising as Nessa popped the cassette into the boom box, hit the play button, and filled the camper with wild beats that made Demelza want to punch the air as if boxing invisible monsters.

Nessa went to Demelza's drawing desk, dipped her finger into a pot of light-blue paint, and drew a war stripe along her left cheek. "Ready?" she asked.

Demelza pulled on her hood, shouldered her backpack, and nodded. They bumped fists.

"Honk!" Captain Honkers was flapping round their ankles as if he knew something exciting was about to happen. Demelza grabbed a pot of red water paint and a paintbrush from the desk, crouched down and painted a large circle on each of his wings. Nessa laughed, then reached for a teddy bear on Demelza's bed, removed the little leather cap and goggles it was wearing, and popped them onto the goose's head. "For protection," she said. Honkers bobbed up and down enthusiastically.

"Honnnk! HONNNK!"

They were ready. Nessa fast-forwarded the tape to a quiet, stealthy-sounding track, then strapped her boom box across her back. Leaving the bedside lamp on in case Demelza's dad looked out at the camper from the house, they slipped outside into the cool night air.

They hopped on their bikes and cycled quietly out of the camper park, passing through the long, creepy shadows of the golf course figures on their way to the cliff overlooking the turrets.

"What do you think?" asked Nessa, stepping out of the way to reveal a long, thin wooden bridge stretching from the cliff to the first turret. "I borrowed your dad's ladder from the shed behind your house and laid a few old planks over the rungs. It's really strong, see?" She stepped onto the bridge and bounced gently up and down.

Demelza tried not to flinch as she imagined both plank and ladder breaking, sending Nessa plunging into the icy water and rocks below.

"Try it," said Nessa, beckoning her onto the bridge.

Demelza bit her lip as she put one foot onto it. The wood creaked loudly underfoot, and she jumped back and shook her head. "I can't," she squeaked, face flushing as she wondered if Nessa thought she was a big chicken.

Nessa stopped bouncing. She came back from the bridge and put her arm around Demelza's shoulder. "Sorry, D. I forgot how frightening it must be for you. We can leave it if you want to. Maybe, if we tell someone about the treasure and they went in for it, they'd give us a cut? Like a finder's fee."

Demelza shook her head. "No. It has to be us. This was the last thing Mom tried to do. We have to finish it. Not even to save the camper park and golf course, but for her."

Nessa chewed her thumbnail and looked across her bridge to the turret. "You really love riding your bike, right?"

"Yeah. It's the best feeling in the world. Like I'm flying, or riding my steed into battle!"

"Okay, so how would you feel about riding your silver

steed over this drawbridge to begin your quest to vanquish your fear, drive out the curse, claim the treasure in the name of your mother, and save your home?"

A flame flickered in Demelza's chest. She stood a little taller, and the thin bridge suddenly looked a bit wider, like a drawbridge inviting them on an adventure. She took a deep breath and clenched her hands by her sides.

"I'll do it!" she said, returning Nessa's joyous high five.

"I'll be right behind you," said Nessa. "I know you can do it, D. You're the awesomest person I know."

Demelza pulled her hood tight around her face to hide her blushes as they picked up their bikes. "Better wheel them back a bit," she said. "I think I'll need a run-up for this."

They wheeled their bikes back from the cliff edge and took up position directly facing Nessa's drawbridge. Nessa's boom box began to play classical music full of dramatic trumpets and violins.

"'Ride of the Valkyries!'" Nessa exclaimed.

Demelza took a deep breath as the music swelled and made her feel a little braver.

"I'll go first," she said.

"Are you sure about this?" asked Nessa.

"A million percent," Demelza said, nodding. "Do you think they'll write music and sing songs about us?"

"If they don't, we'll sing songs about it ourselves," said Nessa. "Ready?"

Demelza wriggled in her saddle and gripped her handlebars tight. "Ready." She raised her fist into the air.

"For Mom!" she shouted.

"For Demelza's mom!" yelled Nessa as they began to pedal like fury.

Demelza led the way, lining the drawbridge up in the center of her handlebars. Her heart was racing as fast as her feet were pedaling. The world dropped away on both sides as she hit the drawbridge. It was only a few feet, but it looked like a mile. She fixed her eyes on the turret, murmuring, "Don't-look-down, don't-look-down," as she flew across the bridge, Nessa right behind her on Neon Justice. The bridge bowed downward a little as she reached the middle, but she kept going. Within seconds she was skidding onto the top of the tower, brakes squealing as her wheels scattered ancient nests to the wind.

The remnants of the castle's battlements stopped both of

them toppling over the edge as Nessa slid into her. The gulls nesting around the tower took off, shrieking angrily at the girls and their noisy music for disturbing their sleep.

"I don't believe it," said Demelza, her eyes shining as she gripped Nessa's arms. "We did it! We're really here, on top of Penfurzy Castle!"

Captain Honkers flapped over to join in the celebrations as they whooped into the wind, hissing at any gulls that dared to try and land near them.

The top of the tower was covered in clumps of grass and weeds, which had taken root in every nook and cranny. The ground was slimy with bird droppings, but Demelza could just about make out something wooden below their feet.

They began to scrape away the mixture of moss, puffin, and seagull poo with the edge of their shoes and found flagstones and a wooden trapdoor. Captain Honkers pattered around them, picking at insects evicted from their homes as the girls dug away. Finally they revealed a large iron ring set into the trapdoor.

"Back, Honkers!" shouted Demelza as the goose launched himself, beak-first, at a worm wriggling out from under the ring. Nessa grabbed the goose and pulled him out of the way as Demelza reached for the ring with her Game Gauntlet. An eggy smell filled her nostrils as murky purple mist hissed into the air, breaking the spell on the castle entrance. Nessa grabbed hold of the ring with her, and, together, they pulled with all their might against the centuries of bird poo that had glued the door shut. Finally, with a sticky grinding sound, the trapdoor began to move.

"HEAVE!" the girls shouted as the trapdoor creaked open to reveal a dark, gaping hole through which the castle seemed to exhale a breath of dank air. It was open to its first visitors in centuries.

Nessa switched off her boom box.

"Stealth mode activated," she said as she slung it across her back.

Demelza cupped Captain Honkers' head in her hands and looked into his eyes through the goggles. "You're on guard, Honkers! Defend the bridge, and our bikes, till your very last honk. If we're not back by dawn, send help. We're counting on you, Captain! We'll see you again soon." As they began to descend into the darkness, Demelza prayed she was telling the truth.

Chapter Eleven
THE PICKLED KNIGHT

The trapdoor banged shut behind Demelza and Nessa with a boom that echoed down the staircase and spiraled into the depths of the castle below them. Demelza switched on the head flashlight she had strapped over her bike helmet as Nessa strapped hers under the shoulder strap of her laser tag breastplate.

The air smelled damp, and the steps were even slimier than the trapdoor. As they made their way round and round and down and down the spiral staircase, they gripped the iron handrail tightly in case their feet flew out from under them—which Demelza's did twice. She was glad she was wearing pads as her elbow hit the hard stone steps, but her grip on the handrail remained tight.

"Which way now?" asked Nessa as they reached the bottom and found themselves in a corner with a corridor branching off to either side of them.

Demelza thumbed through her mom's notebook. "There's nothing in here about the inside of the castle. Mom probably didn't know anything about it. I guess we're on our own now. Which way do you think?"

Nessa shone her flashlight in each direction. Both corridors looked the same—stone walls lined with paintings and tapestries with the occasional suit of armor standing guard over the empty castle. "Either way looks as good as any. We just need to find the stairs down. If the treasure is here, I'm thinking it will either be locked deep down in the darkest cellars"—they both shivered at the thought—"or in the Great Hall."

"Ooh, yes!" said Demelza. "We'll try that first. It's always at the heart of a castle, so it shouldn't be hard to find. I think it's"—she licked her finger and held it in the air, hoping it looked as though she was using deep scientific methods before announcing—"this way. Come on!"

They crept down the branch to their right, the light from their flashlights doing little to chase away the gloom.

"This place is freaky," said Nessa, as her boot crunched down on something that looked suspiciously like a rib bone. "We have to be really careful."

"It even sounds creepy!" said Demelza. "Listen." She cupped her hands around her mouth and shouted "Helloooo!" and put her hand behind her ear as her voice echoed back. *Helloooo-helloooo-helloooo.* Nessa clapped her hand to her head as Demelza's *Helloooo* kept on bouncing, becoming oddly deeper and deeper in tone before finally fading away.

"What did I just say?" whispered Nessa in the silent aftermath of Demelza's yell. "By careful, I also meant quiet, as we don't want to—" She stopped as a couple of lights flared at the end of the corridor.

"Uh-oh, what was that?" said Demelza, straining her eyes to see the source of the light. There was a distant **thwumff** as another two lights appeared a little closer.

"I don't like this," said Nessa as another two flared, closer again.

"The torches!" gasped Demelza as, two by two, the torches mounted on the castle walls burst into flame. The lights drew closer and closer until the torches on the walls either side of

them roared to life. The phenomenon continued down the corridor behind them until the whole place was aglow.

"Well, I guess there's no point creeping around now," sighed Nessa. "Whatever is in this place, it knows we're here."

Even in the warm light of the torches flickering on the walls, Demelza felt the castle was still cold and unwelcoming.

"This is weird," said Nessa as they passed a long, narrow window set deep into the thick wall. "I didn't think they had glass back then." She clambered up onto the deep stone window sill and reached out to touch the glass.

"Holy Honkers," Demelza gasped as her friend's hand disappeared right through it!

"It's water!" said Nessa. "There's no glass, but the sea isn't coming in!"

"Magic!" gasped Demelza, squeezing in next to Nessa and poking her fingers through the window and into the icy sea. "Do you think it's something to do with the curse?" she asked. "Maybe as well as keeping people out, it stops the water from getting in."

"Aargh, gerroff!" said Nessa, trying to pull her arm back inside as though something was tugging on it.

Demelza grabbed her arm and helped her heave, afraid

that her friend was suddenly being attacked by a shark. They both staggered back as Nessa dragged her arm out of the water. Demelza fell off the window ledge when she saw what was biting Nessa's hand.

A human head, blue and wrinkled like old leather, with a curled white beard.

"Ahh! Get-it-off, get-it-off!" cried Nessa, shaking her hand frantically, but the head was clamped firmly to her fingerless, leather glove.

"Ew ew eewwwww!" screamed Demelza, trying not to puke as she grabbed the head by the beard and tried to pry its mouth open.

Nessa leaned back and pulled with all her might until her hand finally slid from her glove, leaving Demelza holding the head by the beard. It opened its eyes and spat out the glove, along with a baby crab. Demelza shrieked, dropped the head, and kicked it away from her.

"That," said the head as it bounced off the opposite wall and rolled a few feet until it was sitting upright on its severed neck, "was extremely rude!"

"Yeargh!" yelled Demelza, drawing her leg back to kick it away again.

"Wait!" said Nessa, grabbing Demelza and yanking her back before she could launch the head down the corridor like a freakish soccer ball.

"Thank you for harnessing your wild beast!" said the head, scowling at Demelza as it tilted to each side to tip sea water out of its ears. "You have my gratitude for rescuing me from my watery grave."

"Uh, you're welcome," said Nessa as Demelza stared unblinkingly at the head, trying hard to remember if she had actually woken up that morning or if she was still in bed dreaming. She slapped herself on the cheek. Nope, definitely awake, she thought.

"What happened to..." Demelza asked. "I mean, where's, y'know..."

"My body?" said the head. "Probably rotting atop one of the towers. I was on lookout duty one day when I heard someone behind me. Before I could say hail, fellow, my head went tumbling down into the sea. There I have bobbed around for centuries, being pickled in the briny blue as I tried to get back inside to warn my brothers of the murderer among us. However, I fear I may be too late. The castle has been dark and silent for the many centuries I have floated around its walls."

"You were one of the Penfurzy knights!" said Nessa.

"Were? I still am!" said the pickled knight. "Being dead doesn't change that. My thanks again, but I have no time to waste jabbering with peasants. I must away to learn what has befallen my brothers." He began to wriggle from side to side, then, with a wet, squelching sound, started to bounce away down the corridor on the stump of his severed neck.

"Do you think we should have asked him about the treasure?" said Nessa as he turned the corner and bounced out of sight, the squelching noise growing fainter and fainter.

"Nope," said Demelza, glad to see the back of the pickled knight, afraid that the squelch would forever haunt her dreams.

They continued down the corridor, the flags and tapestries

that hung from the ceiling and walls fluttering slightly in a breeze that they couldn't feel. Nessa tried each door they passed, but they were either locked tight or the hinges were rusted shut. Demelza gave each suit of armor they passed a wide berth, unable to shake the feeling that they were watching and waiting for a chance to grab her.

"That's weird," said Nessa as they reached the end of the corridor. "We haven't passed any steps. I was sure they would be here."

"Maybe they're hidden behind the tapestry," said Demelza, looking up at the slightly moldy embroidered scene in front of them. It featured a knight astride a rearing horse, busy vanquishing a fire-breathing dragon. Demelza watched as Nessa tried to pull the tapestry aside. It appeared to be glued firmly to the wall.

"Who goes there?" shouted a distant voice.

"Whoa, that was awesome!" said Demelza, impressed with her friend's ventriloquism skills. "Do it again!"

Nessa looked at her, head cocked to one side as though trying to figure out if Demelza was pulling her leg. "That wasn't you?" she asked.

"I said, who goes there!" came the voice again.

"No. Way," said Nessa, staring at the tapestry.

Demelza almost toppled backward as she realized what Nessa was looking at. The knight in the scene had turned his horse and was riding through the tapestry toward them. The little stitches that made up him and his horse seemed to move, as though re-stitching the knight as he rode closer and closer, until he filled up most of the tapestry. Demelza clutched Nessa's arm, ready to run, but it seemed the knight couldn't actually leave the tapestry.

"Name yourselves, interlopers!" he demanded, shaking his spear at them.

"De...Demelza," said Demelza, trying to wrap her head around that fact that she was talking to a tapestry just a few minutes after speaking to a decapitated head.

"And, um, I'm Nessa," said Nessa, prodding at his shifting stitches.

"Unhand me, scoundrel!" said the knight, shifting away from her probing finger. "Well, Demelza, Nessa. I am Sir Cubert, of the Penfurzy knights. Doomed to live within this tapestry since my body's demise, and I demand to know why you are trespassing in this accursed place."

"I, well, we..." began Demelza, not sure how to respond to the needlework knight, who, now she thought about it, looked a bit like a pixelated computer game character.

"Searching for our treasure, no doubt!" he shouted, waving his spear.

"Treasure? What treasure?" asked Nessa innocently, but there was no fooling Sir Cubert.

"There's no fooling me!" he shouted. "I know a greedy treasure hunter when I see one. None have intruded on this place for hundreds of years, but those who did are still rotting here."

"We need the treasure—to save my home!" said Demelza.

"Save? You are foolish indeed. The treasure doesn't save. It brings only misfortune. It turned me and my brothers against one another. For years we had fought together, but once we found that treasure in heathen lands, our brotherhood was torn asunder. We decided to return it to where we found it, but our leader, Sir Warleggan, wouldn't let us, and, one by one, we perished at his hand. He employed dark magic to sink our castle beneath the waves. Our souls have been trapped within this undersea prison for centuries, and will remain here for centuries more."

"But what if we could save you, too?" asked Demelza. She raised her gloved hand. "My gauntlet can banish the curse. It has already saved us from it loads of times."

The knight's head grew bigger in the tapestry as he moved closer to examine the glove. "A curious item. It definitely holds power, but not enough to banish the curse from here where it is strongest." He added in a whisper, "The curse is how the treasure protects itself. The closer you get, the stronger it will be."

"Where is the treasure?" asked Nessa.

"The stairs that will lead you down are behind this impervious tapestry, and I am bound to pose a riddle to all who seek to pass. It must be answered correctly before I can let you through." He leaned forward and murmured through his stitched teeth, "I'll make it an easy one, though."

"And if we don't answer correctly?" asked Nessa.

"Ah. I thought you might ask." He sighed. "Now that's where I can't offer you any help." There was a loud clanking behind them. Demelza's hands flew to her mouth as she turned to see two suits of armor at the far end of the corridor step down from their plinths.

The armor began to march slowly toward them.

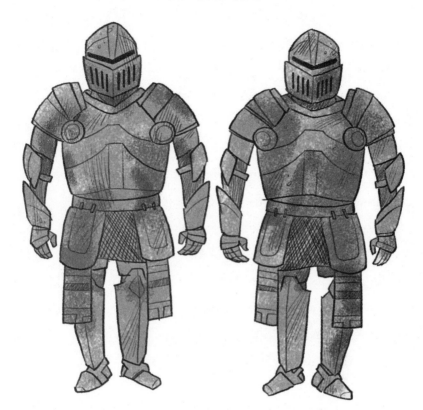

CLANK

CLANK

CLANK

"You must answer correctly before they reach you," said Sir Cubert. "Or you'll end up like the others who failed. Try to force your way through, and the same fate awaits." He nodded toward the closest suit of armor. The visor flicked upward, and Demelza's headlight shone into the helmet, revealing a yellowing human skull. A spider ran out of one eye socket and scurried back into the other. Demelza tried to swallow, but her mouth was completely dry.

"Okay, ask, ASK!" she said as the two suits of armor continued their slow march, one clanking step at a time.

"Ready?" said Sir Cubert.

CLANK
CLANK
CLANK

"Just tell us the riddle!" cried Nessa.

"Okay." The knight cleared his throat:

"You'll find me in jungles, but also in parks.
I'm really quite silent; you won't hear my bark.
I come in all sizes—fat, thin, long, or short.
I can teach you a lesson but cannot be taught.
I'm the stickiest thing in all of the world,
Your best friend is happiest when I am hurled.
Tell me, what am I?"

Demelza's feet started to dance involuntarily under her as the armor clanked closer and closer while she tried to wrap her brain around the riddle.

"Ugh, I don't know!" she cried. "Jungle, bark, sticky. Uh, is it...is it a wolf covered in honey? Do wolves live in the jungle?"

"Is that your answer?" asked Sir Cubert.

"No!" shouted Nessa quickly. "Can we have a clue?"

"I have given you the biggest clue I can."

"Uh, a tiger? A fountain? A ball? Molasses?" said Demelza, rattling off anything she could think of that might be found in a park, jungle, could be thrown, or was sticky. "A Frisbee? A lake? A howler monkey? Glue? A, a, a, a..."

"I believe I was wise not to impose the usual three-guess limit," said Sir Cubert.

The armor kept coming, only about four feet from them now—three feet, two feet.

"A teacher? A frog?" shouted Demelza.

"Shhhhh! Chill out!" said Nessa. "I'm trying to think. Best friend? Like man's best friend—a dog?"

Demelza hopped from foot to foot as the suits of armor opened up to reveal their empty insides. They reached out their hands, ready to grab Nessa and Demelza and to pull them inside and trap them forever.

"When I am hurled...stickiest thing in all of the world," muttered Nessa. "No, it couldn't be that easy, could it?" She frowned.

"Just say it!" screamed Demelza as the gauntlets reached out for their shoulders.

Nessa looked up at Sir Cubert. "A...a stick?"

The armor froze. Demelza held her breath as they paused for what seemed like forever, then retracted their hands, turned and marched back up the corridor. Demelza's jelly legs finally gave out. She sank to the floor, dragging Nessa with her.

"Well done!" said Sir Cubert, clapping his hands together. "You may proceed on your quest. I wish you more luck than myself and my brothers." He leaned forward and muttered, "Just watch out for Sir Warleggan. He brought the curse upon us, and now it seeps out from this place. Soon it will infect the entire land."

Before they could ask anything more, the tapestry swung aside, revealing another dark spiral staircase.

Demelza and Nessa stepped through, and the tapestry

dropped back down behind them. Demelza prodded it and found it to be as hard as stone. The way out was sealed; there was no turning back.

Chapter Twelve
METAL MITTS

The darkness seemed almost thick enough to touch now, and Demelza and Nessa's flashlights barely lit their path as they descended toward the heart of the castle.

"He didn't really mean that, did he?" asked Demelza. "About the curse infecting Penfurzy?" Her mind flashed back to the strange way Mrs. Henwood had acted in the park with the sparrows, and Mr. Par and Mr. Lanner chasing the squirrel on the tor.

"Well, look at the cursed items we've come across so far," said Nessa. "And I wouldn't be surprised if it's starting to leak out from this place if it's been here for centuries. You'd better keep that glove of yours handy!"

"You don't think this Sir Warleggan is still here, do you?" asked Demelza.

"He'll be long dead," said Nessa. "If he is here, he's probably trapped in a tapestry or something like Sir Cubert. I doubt he could hurt us."

Demelza noticed the uncertainty in her voice. "Ow! What did you stop for?" she asked, walking into Nessa's back as her friend stopped on the stairs.

"Shh! Can you hear that?"

Demelza cupped her hand behind her ear. There was a metallic skittering noise, like someone wearing thimbles and tapping their fingers. "Where is that coming from?" She turned her head to shine her headlight up, down, and around the narrow staircase.

"I don't know, but let's hurry," said Nessa.

They linked arms and doubled their pace, Demelza holding tight to the handrail while rushing down the wider side of the steps, Nessa turning her feet sideways to stabilize herself on the narrow inner edge. But the skittering was getting louder. It now sounded like lots of hands wearing lots and lots of thimbles.

"Whoa, hold on!" shouted Nessa, tripping on the narrow inner stairs as Demelza began to run. Demelza stopped and grabbed for Nessa, but it was too late to break her fall, and they both went tumbling together down the remaining half-dozen steps.

"I think I broke my butt bone!" said Demelza, rubbing her bottom.

Nessa groaned as she sat up and examined her scraped arms in the light of Demelza's headlamp, her own smashed in the fall. "There! What was that!" she shouted suddenly.

Demelza yelped as Nessa grabbed her by her frizzy bunches and moved her head up and down and left and right like a searchlight as something skittered around, trying to stay in the shadows.

"Ahh!" cried Demelza as the creature finally froze in the center of the pool of light cast upward by the flashlight. "A giant metal spider!"

"Five legs?" counted Nessa. "That's not a spider!" It crouched against the ceiling and began to wiggle. "It's an armored glove. D, watch out!"

Nessa rolled out of the way as the metal glove pounced. It glanced off her plastic breastplate and smacked into Demelza's shoulder, knocking her back down onto the floor. As she tried to get up, it scrambled to her neck and closed its cold fingers around her throat.

"Get it off!" she gasped, as the glove began to squeeze.

"Leave her alone!" shouted Nessa, grasping its little finger and pulling back hard until it began to peel away from Demelza's neck.

Demelza grabbed at the metal glove with her Game Gauntlet and squeezed, feeling it begin to weaken.

"Hold tight!" said Nessa as the glove began to shake in Demelza's hand. The metal fingers splayed out as the familiar smelly mist began to drift from its joints until, finally, the last traces of the curse drifted away.

"Sir Cubert was right," said Demelza, shaking the dead metal glove so that the fingers flopped around uselessly, then dropping it to the floor. "The curse is much stronger here. I didn't think that was going to work."

"Well, it had better keep working," said Nessa, "'cause reinforcements are on the way!"

Demelza squeaked as she looked up, her headlight casting huge spidery shadows across the walls as a dozen or more metal gloves scuttled toward them from the stairs, walls, and ceiling. She scrabbled in her backpack and threw two water pistols to Nessa, drawing two of her own and pointing them at the advancing gauntlets.

The metal gloves slowed their advance a little as the girls kept their pistols trained on them. Nessa and Demelza backed out of the stairwell and reversed into what seemed to be the castle's kitchens. The gloves swarmed through the doorway after them and took up crouched positions on the walls and ceilings, each raising two fingers like antennae as though trying to sense what the girls would do.

"Ready..." whispered Nessa.

"Aim..." said Demelza.

"FIRE!" they both yelled as the first metal glove dropped from the ceiling and galloped toward them. The first spray of water hit it as it leapt into the air. It gave a metallic screech, then flopped onto its back, fingers curling up like a dying spider as it rusted stiff in the streams from four water pistols. Mist hissed from its joints.

"Uh-oh, here we go!" said Nessa, pulling Demelza close so that they stood back-to-back as the rest of the gloves advanced, dropping from the ceiling, scuttling across the floor and walls and launching themselves toward the girls. Demelza's and Nessa's arms whirled as they took down their metal foes one by one, rusting them to a standstill.

"I'm nearly out of water," Nessa shouted back as another glove curled up with a screech.

"Me too," said Demelza, shaking her pistols and hearing

very little water sloshing around inside. She looked around wildly. There was nowhere to fill them in the medieval kitchen, and not even a window to stick them out of so they could fill up with sea water. There were still at least seven metal mitts left. They had been holding off and circling warily, but seemed to realize the girls were no longer firing so wildly. They began to edge closer.

"I've got two water balloons in my backpack," said Demelza softly, "and I might be able to hold them back with my Game Gauntlet, too. You're the fastest runner. Do you think you can get to a window to fill your pistols?"

"You've been carrying full water balloons in your backpack? Why would—" said Nessa, before seeming to realize this wasn't the time for that conversation. "Okay, I'll be as quick as I can!" The gloves were blocking the bottom of the staircase, so Nessa ran for the double doors at the back of the room, emptying the last of her water onto a metal mitt that had foolishly broken off from the others to chase her.

"It's locked!" she shouted back to Demelza as she shook the handles, then kicked the doors.

"We're done for!" shouted Demelza as a glove leapt for her face. She hurled one of her water balloons, hitting it in its palm.

The balloon exploded, sending out splashes of water, which sent all of the others skittering back. The glove dropped to the ground, a rusted lump.

"I've got an idea!" called Nessa. She put down her boom box, grabbed a handful of fridge magnets from her backpack and hurled them at the mitts. "That should keep them busy for a while," she said as she disappeared under the huge kitchen table.

The magnets stuck fast to the metal gloves, clinging to their fingers and in between their joints. Demelza laughed as one began leaping around like a buckaroo as it tried to flip a Blackpool Tower magnet from its back. The others were rolling around in circles trying to scrape off magnets shaped like a puffin, Penfurzy's tor, a crab, a Penfurzy knight, a sheep, the Union Jack, a fish, a bottle of tomato sauce, a wedge of cheese... Finally the mitts began working together to pull the magnets off each other and flick them across the room.

When they were finally free of the clinging magnets, the gloves turned their attention to Demelza. Now that she was on her own, they began edging warily toward her.

"Nessa..." she called.

"One minute!" Nessa called back from under the table.

"But..."

"Just hold them off a bit longer."

"Hurry!"

"Don't rush me, D. This is a dangerous operation!"

The gloves were getting closer.

What was Nessa doing? Demelza wondered if she had decided to abandon her by hiding under the table until the metal gloves had gone. She brandished her last water balloon and hurled it at the glove that had crept the closest. It bounced over it and landed in the center of the mitts, splashing all of them at once. Little orange rust spots appeared across the gloves, but it wasn't nearly enough to stop them. She leapt up onto the table as they realized she was now unarmed and cantered toward her.

She pulled the plunger out of her

backpack and tried to wave them off, but they began clambering up the table legs. She slammed the plunger down onto one and hurled it at the wall, then grabbed another from her shoulder and held onto it with her Game Gauntlet as it screeched and wriggled. The other gloves clung to her feet, trying to pull her over.

"Nesssaaaaa!" she screamed, trying to kick them off.

"Get away from her, you mitts!" roared Nessa as she slid out from under the table. She was brandishing a bottle in each hand, foam fizzing out from under the lids as she shook them vigorously. "Get down, D!" she yelled. Demelza finished throttling the mist out of the glove she was holding, then dropped to the ground. Nessa hurled the bottles, then threw herself over Demelza and covered her ears.

The bottles exploded the second they hit the ground, sending a sticky, fizzy, crackling foam spraying across the room and over every gauntlet. The mitts squealed and raced away as fast as they could, mist trailing behind them as they fell apart and rusted to orange dust. Soon there was nothing left but rust, departing mist, and echoing death screeches.

"That was amazing!" said Demelza, surveying the damage Nessa's grenades had wreaked. "What was that?"

"Pop Rocks and soda," said Nessa, wiping her sticky hands on her jeans.

"Whoa!" said Demelza. "Connan Lenteglos said you can die if you eat Pop Rocks then drink soda!"

"I saw a kid explode when he tried it," said Nessa, nodding sagely. "Hey, look, the doors are opening now!"

"That's weird," said Demelza as she watched them swing open. "It's like when you're playing Mutant Renegade Queens and get trapped in the sewers until you beat all the robo-rats."

"Yeah, this whole place is playing games with us," said Nessa. "The sooner we find the treasure, the sooner we can get out of here!"

After passing through the rest of the kitchens, a storeroom full of wine barrels, and an entrance hall, they found themselves in a long gallery. The walls bore a dozen portraits of what had to be more Penfurzy knights, all staring down from their paintings in proud and surly silence. Demelza didn't like the way they all seemed to be glaring at her.

"Isn't it weird the way the eyes seem to follow you around the room?" she said as they tiptoed through the gallery, keeping an eye out for scuttling metal gloves or hungry suits of armor.

"Um, yeah," said Nessa. "Except these ones actually are following us."

Demelza stopped and looked at the nearest painting. It showed a knight with flowing blond hair who was wearing an impractical-looking gold helmet with a plume of multi-colored feathers. "Sir Launceston," she read from a plaque on the frame. She moved from side to side in front of the painting, and her toes curled up inside her trainers as the eyes followed her.

"Go home!" shouted Sir Launceston, so suddenly and so loudly that Demelza almost jumped up into Nessa's arms.

Every painting in the gallery immediately sprang to life, the knights all shouting at the top of their voices:

"BEGONE!"

Nessa and Demelza clutched at each other as the paintings ranted, yelled, and cursed at them, filling the gallery with so much noise Demelza felt her head was going to burst.

"ENOUUUUGH!" bellowed Nessa at last.

"Yeah, shut it!" joined in Demelza. "Or else!"

The paintings stopped shouting and stared down at them, as though surprised the girls hadn't run screaming from the room.

"Or else what?" asked a heavyset knight with thick black

eyebrows, leaning his painted face slightly out of his frame to see them better.

"Or...or else I'll unblock your face!" said Demelza, waving her toilet plunger threateningly. "And Nessa will explode you with her soda grenades!"

Nessa pulled out a little bottle and packet of popping candy and waved them threateningly. The knights looked baffled.

"I have no idea what you're saying, imp," said the knight.

"I'm saying, we already shot, strangled, and bombed the curse out of a load of metal spider gloves," said Demelza. "We're not scared of you."

"Okay, okay," said Sir Launceston quickly.

"No need for violence."

He ducked far back into his painting and seemed to have a conversation with the other knights behind the wall.

"Sir Bude," the knight with the thick black eyebrows introduced himself with a little salute as he leaned out of his painting.

"Are you telling us that you vanquished the metal mitts of mayhem?"

"Vanquished them to dust!" said Demelza, making a fist with her Game Gauntlet as Nessa blew on the barrels of her pistols.

"And we solved Sir Cubert's daft riddle and saved ourselves from being eaten by the armor upstairs."

"'Tis true!" said a voice, accompanied by a loud squelching as the pickled knight bounced into the room.

"Sir Calenick?" said Sir Bude. "Where've you been hiding?"

"Hiding? Hiding!" yelled the head.

"I've been bobbing around with the fishes for centuries after my head was hacked from my body as I bravely guarded our fortress! But I am here at last, my brothers in arms. Here to warn you that there is..." he paused dramatically, "a murderer among us!"

The knights looked at each other, then back at Sir Calenick's head.

"Um, we know," said Sir Launceston. "We're all dead. The curse is keeping our souls trapped in our paintings."

"Oh. Right," said the pickled knight. "In that case we must find whoever was responsible and—"

"Sir Warleggan," said Sir Bude.

"Yup, 'twas Sir Warleggan," echoed all of the other paintings.

"Ah, I see," said the head, looking down at the floor.

"But we really appreciate the warning," said Sir Launceston sincerely.

The pickled knight sniffed. "Well, at least I can inform you that these peasants are telling the truth. They have shown both wit and bravery."

Sir Bude and the knights were now looking at Nessa and Demelza with something like admiration in their painted faces.

"Could they be the ones foretold to break the curse?" asked Sir Launceston.

"The Imp and the Trespasser?" said the pickled knight.

"Hey, I'm not an imp! I'm just short for my age!" said Demelza.

"And I'm not a trespasser," said Nessa.

"Well, we are kind of trespassing here," said Demelza.

"And you did break into my camper. Not that I mind!" she added quickly as Nessa gave her a little glare.

A red-haired knight piped up from a frame labeled SIR BODMIN. "When we acquired the treasure in another land, a priestess at one of the tombs we stole from—"

The hall erupted in a cacophony of coughs as the other knights tried to get his attention.

"Uh, I mean one of the grateful people who gave it to us, said that a curse would turn us against each other, and, one by one, we would fall until only one remained. She said that our souls would be trapped in a fate worse than death until the Trespasser and the Imp arrived. Only they can break the curse and free our souls from this place, so that we may rest in peace at last. Could that really be you? Have you come to save us?"

"Maybe," said Nessa. "So, if you could just point us in the direction of the treasure, we'll get on with our quest."

"Your quest being to free our souls, not to claim the treasure and desert us, right?" said Sir Launceston.

"Absolutely," said Nessa. "We, uh, just need to see the treasure so that, so that..."

"...so that we can figure out the best way to break the curse and free you," finished Demelza.

"Hmm, well, I suppose that sounds logical," said Sir Launceston, still looking at them through narrowed eyes. He pointed down the gallery. "It's through there."

"Thanks!" said Demelza, skipping toward the double doors at the end of the room.

"Wait!" called Sir Bodmin. "Sir Warleggan may be in there, too. He murdered every one of us—"

"Except me!" shouted a young black-haired knight on the

opposite wall. "You murdered me while I was sitting in the garderobe."

"And for that I have apologized a thousand times, Sir Alturnun! As I was saying, he murdered nearly every one of us and is still very dangerous. None of us have seen him in over a century, but he won't leave the treasure unguarded. You would do well to keep your eyes peeled for traps. Like that one." He nodded toward the doors Demelza was just reaching for. Two giant blades suddenly swung down from the ceiling, creating a rush of air that blew back Demelza's hair. The blades crossed in front of the doors before sweeping back upward. "We'll disable it for you. Just make sure you fulfill your destiny and set us free."

"We will not fail you, brave knights!" said Demelza, saluting them and keeping a suspicious eye on the ceiling for more swinging blades as Nessa hurried her through the doors.

"Good luck!" shouted the knights as one.

"You'll need it," Demelza heard the pickled knight mutter behind them.

Chapter Thirteen
SIR WARLEGGAN

Demelza blinked, then blinked again, as an amazing sight met her eyes. They were staring at a mountain of treasure—coins of all sizes, goblets, jeweled rings, necklaces, crowns, ornate boxes and trinkets—all gleaming gold. She wondered if she could dive into the pile and swim through it, just like she'd seen in cartoons.

"Wait!" called Nessa as Demelza ran for the treasure. "The curse! Remember?"

Demelza stopped herself at the last minute, arms pinwheeling as she leaned back to avoid touching anything. She reached down with her Game Gauntlet and prodded a jewel-encrusted goblet that was sticking out of the pile. Nothing happened.

"I think it's okay," she said, picking up a few gold coins in the glove and tossing one to Nessa. "See?"

Nessa made no move to catch it.

The coin bounced off her cheek but she didn't even seem to notice. She was staring at something else. Demelza followed her gaze up to a throne standing high at the other end of the hall. Sitting on it, wearing an armored breastplate and a golden crown, was the skeleton of the tallest person Demelza had ever seen.

"Sir Warleggan?" she whispered to Nessa. The whisper took on a life of its own as it left her lips, repeating like an echo and spreading to fill every corner of the huge room.

"SirWarlegganSirWarlegganSirWarlegganSirWarleggan," swirled the whisper. The skeleton began to shudder. Its bones clacked. It sat up straight and began to shimmer as a ghostly body began to form around it. Soon the bones were covered in glowing skin that lit the hall with a creepy, green glow. Demelza stared up at the man now sitting on the throne: a knight with a terrible-looking sword and an even more terrible sneer on his scarred face.

Demelza edged closer to Nessa as the knight rose from his throne, leaving glowing trails in the air behind him. He stretched, brushed the dust from his armored shoulders, then lazily descended the stairs toward them.

"I am Sir Warleggan," he said, raising his sword and pointing it at them. "Lord of this castle, mightiest of all the Penfurzy knights, scourge of evil-doers, righter of wrongs, and"—he glared at the coins held in Demelza's gauntlet—"protector of this treasure."

"Huh-hi," gulped Demelza, quickly dropping the coins back onto the pile and giving the knight an awkward wave. "Um, I'm Demelza Penrose and this is—"

"Silence!" roared Sir Warleggan. "I care not who you are, only that you came here to steal from me."

Demelza took a step back as the knight advanced. "Sorry, sir. We weren't stealing. We was just borrowing so we can save my home. My dad has to sell it, so we thought the treasure would help him. You have so much, and we only need a teensy-weensy little bit."

Sir Warleggan didn't appear to be listening as he marched straight through the pile of treasure. His eyes glowed a dim red as he stopped before them, raised his sword and hissed, "Thieves!"

"Okay, we'll be off now!" said Demelza quickly, pulling on Nessa's sleeve.

But Nessa wasn't budging. Her arms were folded across her

chest as she glared up at the knight. "Is it still classed as stealing if you're taking from a thief?" she asked.

"What?" said Sir Warleggan, pausing.

"What are you doing, Nessa?" Demelza whispered out of the corner of her mouth. "Don't annoy the skeleton with the big sword!"

"A dead thief at that," continued Nessa. "And how can you be a righter of wrongs when you looted all of this from tombs?"

"Looted? How dare you! I have never—"

"And you didn't even give it back when the curse made you kill all of your friends," said Nessa, before leaning over and whispering, "Or did you enjoy killing them all?"

Demelza heard a few whoops from the paintings in the gallery behind them.

"Well spoken, Trespasser!" called the pickled knight.

"Of course I didn't enjoy it! I mean, I didn't kill anyone. Well, they would have killed me if I hadn't," said Sir Warleggan, sword drooping slightly.

"Yeah!" said Demelza. "And how can you be the scourge of evil-doers when you look like you're going to slice us into little bitty pieces with that sword? Seems to me like you're the evil one."

"Evil? I am not evil. I am a Penfurzy knight!" Sir Warleggan shouted, so loudly that the chandeliers began to swing, dislodging generations of spider webs. "One of the most chivalrous, virtuous knights in all of the world!"

"Waving that sword at us isn't very chivalrous," said Demelza. "Aren't knights supposed to put their coats on puddles,

an' give roses to fair maidens after jousts?"

The knight stared dazedly at his sword as if this wasn't going at all as planned.

"And murdering all your fellow knights certainly doesn't sound very chivalrous to me," said Nessa. "What did you do that for?"

"Well, I had to. They wanted to take the treasure back to—"

"Where? Wherever it belonged?" said Demelza.

"It seems to me this treasure has brought you nothing but bad luck," said Nessa. "If me and Demelza take it off your hands, then you might finally be able to rest in peace. It's not like you're doing anything with it. Wouldn't you like to leave this cold, damp castle?"

Demelza thought the knight looked a little smaller and less solid as he bowed his head, seemingly lost in thought. She spotted her opportunity and edged forward, picking up a handful of coins and moving to slip them into her pocket.

Sir Warleggan's head snapped back up to face her. "Thieves!" he screamed.

Demelza dropped the coins in fright.

"Villains!" he shrieked so loudly the whole castle shook. "Witches, wooing me with your words when all you want is my treasure. Well, let's see just how much you want it!"

"Uh-oh. That doesn't sound good," said Nessa as Sir Warleggan raised his arms. The treasure pile began to shake and jingle. Little coins floated up into the air, followed by large jewels, goblets, and trinkets.

"Calm down," said Demelza, backing away from the jingling cloud of gold that was now hovering around the knight. "We're leaving now."

"Oh, it's too late for that," bellowed Sir Warleggan. "There's space for two more paintings in my gallery. Your souls will be trapped here for all eternity!"

"Yeah, but no can do!" said Nessa, grabbing Demelza's hand. They ran for the door to the gallery as all of the paintings called to them to run faster.

BOOM! The doors slammed shut in front of them.

Demelza and Nessa dashed around the hall, but every door out of the room slammed with a bang just before they got to it. Sir Warleggan was toying with them. He waved his arm and a shower of coins flew straight at them. Nessa shoved Demelza to the floor, and the coins thudded into the door behind them so hard that they stuck fast. Demelza looked at the coins, then at Nessa.

"I know," said Nessa. "BOOK IT!"

They leapt to their feet and sprinted around the hall again, ducking and diving as the knight sent floating clusters of treasure hurtling toward them to crash into the walls as they sprang out of the way.

"Aargh!" yelled Demelza as a coin whizzed past her, scratching her cheek and drawing drops of blood.

"Grab a shield!" called Nessa, yanking one from a suit of armor. Demelza looked around, but there was only one suit of armor nearby. A large jewel-encrusted tray teetering on the treasure pile caught her eye. She slammed her toilet plunger onto the back of it with a loud farty squelch, then held it up, using the plunger as a handle.

CLANG! went the tray-shield as a hail of coins glanced off it.

Demelza scuttled over to

Nessa and they held up their shields side by side, creating a wall to protect them against Sir Warleggan's ferocious barrage. The whole room was now covered in coins and bent and broken goblets and jewelry. Demelza's tray-shield was pitted with dents, and her arms were tiring as she struggled to keep it held aloft. The knight had shed much of his armor and half his human form. His bottom half was now only long, ghostly tendrils as he floated around the room, hurling even more golden trinkets down at them.

"Maybe we can hide in that," said Nessa, nodding toward a large gold box that had been uncovered at the bottom of the scattered treasure pile. Two golden figures crouched on either side of the lid, their eagle wings stretched out toward each other. Coins rained down on the shields as they held them over their heads and scurried, like beetles, over to the box.

"It looks Egyptian!" gasped Demelza from under cover of their shields as she ran her fingers over the strange symbols that covered it. "What if there's a mummy in it?"

"Then we'd better hope they don't mind sharing!" said Nessa, standing up to bat a golden crown back at Sir Warleggan with her shield. "Quick, let's get it open."

"I'm not sure that's a good idea," said Demelza. The symbols seemed to be shifting and moving as she watched them, and she could feel the box vibrating under her fingers.

"Leave that alone!" roared Sir Warleggan, spotting Demelza testing the box for the curse with her Game Gauntlet. The ghostly knight whirled around the room, swooping close to them, then zooming away to rain down more treasure as they strained to push open the lid.

"You know what?" panted Nessa as they pushed and pulled at the immensely heavy lid. "I think he can't come too close to us. I reckon he's afraid of your gauntlet."

"Afraid?" bellowed the knight, diving down, then veering away as Demelza held up her Game Gauntlet. "Your gauntlet may hold power, but it can't protect you from being crushed to a pulp!" He raised his arms, and treasure streamed toward him and began to form a gigantic cloud over their heads.

"It's no good!" shouted Nessa as the lid moved by the tiniest fraction. "It's too heavy. We'll never open it!"

"We're doomed!" cried Demelza. "Doooomed!"

Sir Warleggan cackled down at them as he made a hurling motion with his arms. Demelza and Nessa clung together as several tons of gold dropped toward them.

"Goodbye, Nessa," said Demelza, hugging her tight.

"Nice knowing you, D," said Nessa, hugging her back. They both closed their eyes, ready for certain death.

It didn't come. Instead there was a sudden flash of light so bright that it shone through Demelza's closed eyelids.

She opened one eye, then wished she hadn't. The golden lid was hovering five feet above the box. The treasure Sir Warleggan had tried to crush them with was suspended, completely still, in the air. A thick, murky mist was beginning to flow out of the box, pouring down the sides like a slow waterfall. "Nooo!" screamed the knight, staring down into the box. His treasure cloud flew in

182

all directions
across the room and rained
harmlessly to the ground.

"The curse!" shouted Demelza,
grasping Nessa's hand. They scurried back from the path of the
pooling, swirling mist, but it didn't follow them. Its attention, if a mist
could pay attention, seemed to be entirely focused on the knight.

"No! Get back!" shouted Sir Warleggan as a tentacle of mist
shot up, like the arm of an octopus, and seized him by the ankle.

Demelza was transfixed by the way Sir Warleggan was struggling furiously in the air as more tentacles grasped his arms and
legs. Even though he was half transparent, they seemed able to
hold him tight. He began to whimper.

"That box. It must be the source of the curse," said Nessa
as the tentacles began to draw the knight slowly down. "It must
have been leaking out for centuries, and we've just set it free."

"Say you're sorry! Tell it you'll give the treasure back!" Demelza shouted up at the screaming knight.

"It wasn't me; it was them!" said the knight, waving his arms to throw open the doors to the Long Gallery. "They took it. They wouldn't let me return it. Take them, not me!"

Demelza jumped as all of the paintings shouted at once, denying Sir Warleggan's claims and declaring their innocence, but the mist seemed to know the truth. It kept on reeling the knight in, closer and closer. Demelza knew that whatever awaited him in the box wasn't going to be pleasant.

"Just tell it you don't want the treasure," yelled Nessa. "It's no use to you, anyway. It's just keeping your soul trapped here."

"Let it go!" shouted Demelza, the paintings in the gallery all joining it.

"Apologize!" called Sir Bude.

"Give up the treasure!" shouted Sir Bodmin.

"Release us from the curse! Set our souls free!" called the pickled knight.

Sir Warleggan had stopped writhing and seemed to be drawing himself back together, becoming larger and more solid as he pulled back against the force of the tentacles.

"Never!" he roared, his greed overcoming his fear. "I apologize to no one. You will never take my treasure from me!"

The second the words left his ghostly lips, there was a peal of thunder from the box.

"Bad move," said Nessa as a spinning pillar of mist poured out of the box like a tornado. Sir Warleggan screeched, his body stretching as it was sucked into the top of the column until all that could be seen was his screaming head before that, too, was enveloped in the cursed mist. With a *POOF!* the mist rolled back into the box, and the lid dropped back down with a boom, leaving nothing of Sir Warleggan but a lingering scream.

Chapter Fourteen
THE CURSE

Demelza turned to look into the gallery of knights as it exploded with cheers.

"He's gone! Gone forever!" shouted the knights, punching the air and leaning out of their paintings to hug each other, painted tears of joy dripping from the artworks and onto the stone floor.

"Calm yourselves, brothers," called the pickled knight as he bounced away from the pooling tears. "For it seems we are still here, and just as accursed."

"What do you think happened to him?" asked Demelza.

"I'd rather not think about it," said Nessa. "Idiot. All he had to do was give up the treasure, and I bet they'd all be free."

Demelza stared at the mountain of treasure. "There's so much of it," she said. "We wouldn't need much to save my home and the golf course. I bet it wouldn't matter if we just took a tiny little bit."

"I wouldn't do that, D," said Nessa as Demelza reached down and scooped up a handful of gold and jewels.

"See?" said Demelza, casting a glance at the box. "It's fine."

"Seriously, I wouldn't risk it," said Nessa. "Just leave it."

Demelza looked at her, then at the gold in her hands. "I have to. Dad needs it." She shoved the gold into her anorak pockets. "That's all I'm taking. See, we're not greedy, not like he was. Come on, let's get back. Honkers will be getting worried."

The second they turned to leave the hall, a loud rumbling began. Demelza could feel it through the bottom of her feet to the very top of her head. She turned, slowly, to face the box. It had begun to vibrate again.

"It's angry," said Nessa. "I really think you should put the treasure back."

"I can't," said Demelza, clutching her heavy pockets. "We worked so hard to find it!"

Slowly, the lid of the box rose into the air. Dark mist began to pour out, swirling across the floor toward their feet, blocking their path from the room.

"Please!" Demelza shouted at the advancing mist. "Dad needs it. We can't lose our home!"

"Just give it back, D!" pleaded Nessa.

The mist reared up like a seething wave. Demelza put her hand out in front of her face and turned away as it came crashing down. There was a gasp from Nessa. Demelza looked up. The mist was glancing off her glove as though it had hit a glass dome.

"Quick, let's get to the door!" said Nessa, crouching behind her. Demelza headed for the door to the gallery, pushing against the mist with her glove as though walking into a strong wind. The mist kept sending out little tendrils to tug at the gauntlet; they flinched back as though stung at first, but seemed to get braver until Demelza could feel them tugging the glove from her hand.

"Nearly there," said Nessa encouragingly as they pushed closer to the door to freedom. Demelza clenched her fingers tight and held onto the inside of the glove, but it was no use. She gave one last tug but the mist was too strong: the gauntlet slid from her hand, and she fell back onto Nessa as the glove was hurled across the room.

"Oof! Right on my boom box!" squeaked Nessa as she

landed on the cassette player. A blast of rock music filled the hall as her mixtape began playing at full volume. She mouthed something over the deafening noise.

"WHAT?" yelled Demelza, her words lost in the booming beats. She watched Nessa's lips.

"Look at the mist."

She looked. Each bass beat was driving the mist back so that it pulsed around them as it tried and failed to reach them.

"Go!" mouthed Nessa.

They dashed the last few feet to the gallery, the mist pursuing, but unable to get close. The second Demelza dived through the doorway there was a cry from Nessa. She turned to see her friend trapped on the other side of the door as the huge blades began to swing, too fast and far too sharp to risk a leap between them.

"You stopped them before," Demelza cried to the paintings as she watched Nessa hold her boombox up to drive back the mist. "Stop them again, please!"

"You said you would set us free us, Imp," said Sir Bodmin, glaring accusingly.

"You've got to save her!" said Demelza, dropping to her knees and pleading with the pickled knight.

"Like you're saving us? Sneaking away with that gold in your pocket?" said Sir Alturnun behind her. The music from Nessa's boombox was beginning to sound slow and distorted.

"The batteries," called Nessa. "They won't last much longer. I'm going to run for it!"

"No, you'll be cut in two!" screamed Demelza. She turned again to the pickled knight. "Please!" she begged. "Let her in."

"You can save her yourself," said the head.

Demelza thrust her hands into her pockets and drew out the gold and jewels, taking one last glance at her only hope for saving her home.

"You know what you have to do," said Sir Bude.

"Okay, I'm giving it back!" Demelza yelled as the boom box batteries died and the mist closed in on Nessa. "Please. Just leave her alone!" She hurled the gold between the blades and into the heart of the mist. For a second it looked as though Nessa was going to suffer the same fate as Sir Warleggan, but the mist rolled back and slowly began to retreat. The blades stopped swinging, and Demelza threw her arms around Nessa as she dropped her boom box in relief.

"I'm sorry," said Demelza, burying her face in Nessa's jacket. "I shouldn't have taken it."

"It's okay," panted Nessa, patting her on the back. "You had to try."

They watched as the mist swirled around the box, but it didn't disappear inside as it had after it took Sir Warleggan. It seemed to be waiting for something.

"What's it doing?" asked Demelza. "I gave the treasure back."

"Maybe...maybe that's not enough," said Nessa slowly. She turned to the paintings in the gallery. "Sir Warleggan couldn't let go," she said to the paintings. "But what about you? Do you all give up your claim to this treasure that has cursed you all and kept you trapped here?"

"We do!" shouted all of the knights at once. "We don't want it, take it back!"

"And are you sorry you took it?" she asked.

"Very sorry! Oh, so sorry!" shouted the knights.

"What about you?" Nessa asked the pickled knight, who had remained silent and seemed to be avoiding eye contact.

"Sir Calenick!" shouted Sir Bude. "You renounce the treasure at once, or we'll have the Imp throw you back off the tower to live with the crabs and eels."

"I can do that," grinned Demelza, reaching for the pickled knight's ears.

"Okay, I renounce the treasure and extend my sincerest apologies," mumbled the head, without sounding particularly sincere at all.

"We're sorry too," Demelza shouted to the mist. "I only took it to save our home, but I was selfish. The treasure doesn't belong to me, just like it didn't belong to them."

"We'd return it, only we don't know where it came from," said Nessa.

"An' we don't have a ship to sail in, not since Nessa's pirate ship sank. But, if there's a way to give it back, just tell us, if you can."

The mist began to shimmer as the murky, greeny-gray shades turned to a golden glow. The eggy stench Demelza had grown used to faded and became something else.

"Mmm, comic books and poster paint," said Demelza, taking a deep breath.

"Freshly pressed vinyl and new trainers," said Nessa, filling her lungs with the scent.

"Newly forged swords and a bloody battlefield at dawn," said Sir Bude fondly.

"Lady Eowyn's hair," sighed the pickled knight. "I wonder if she still likes short men?" he mused hopefully.

The mist hovered over the treasure pile as the hoard began to disintegrate into golden dust and stream toward the sweet-smelling mist, forming a huge, shimmering cloud. When every last coin had disappeared, the mist flowed back into the box, and the lid dropped down with a boom. There was a high-pitched fizzing noise as the box began to fold in on itself, growing smaller and smaller until, POOF, it disappeared with a tiny ping.

"Where did it go?" asked Demelza.

"Back to wherever it belonged," said Nessa. "So, I guess that's it. The curse has gone." She cocked her head. "What's that noise?"

Demelza cupped her hand behind her ear and heard it, too. A rushing, swooshing, roaring noise that seemed to be getting louder. There was a sudden pop, and the roaring noise filled the hall as the frothing sea began to pour in through the windows.

"The curse has gone!" repeated Demelza as the castle began to shake. "That means the magic seal on the windows has gone too!"

Something else was happening to the castle. Candles dropped from the iron chandeliers as the whole building shook.

"We've got to get out of here!" Nessa yelled, grabbing her boom box and slinging it across her back.

They ran from the hall as ice-cold sea water began to flow over their feet. The ghosts of the knights were flowing out of their paintings as the two girls ran back through the gallery.

"Free! We're free!" they shouted, finally released from their imprisonment.

Demelza could hear the knights calling after them as they fled through the gallery:

"Thank you!"

"Farewell!"

"Godspeed!"

"Fair Eowyn, we shall be reunited at last!" cried the pickled knight as he floated past, his head beginning to shimmer.

Demelza reached out to stop herself tumbling into a wall as the castle continued to shake and rumble—sea water flowing in from every window.

"It's sinking!" she shouted over the roar.

"We need to get back to the top of the tower," Nessa yelled back as they skidded into the entrance hall, waded through the storeroom and splashed through the kitchens.

The water was getting higher. By the time they reached the bottom of the spiral stairs, it had reached Demelza's waist. She had to cling to Nessa as they waded forward against the current.

"It's a waterfall!" said Demelza as a torrent of water began to rush down the stairs.

"That must mean it's no longer closed off at the top," said Nessa. "We can get out!" She pulled a rope from her backpack, and they quickly lashed their waists together before beginning the perilous climb up the stairs. Hand over hand, they pulled themselves up by the handrail. Demelza's legs were heavy under her waterlogged clothes, and the flow of water threatened to sweep her to her doom at any moment. There was a crashing and banging from above. Before Demelza could shout a warning, a jumble of armor came tumbling down the stairs, crashing into Nessa.

Demelza yelped as Nessa lost her grip on the handrail, and the rope binding them together pulled tight as she flailed around in the water, trying to get a foot- or handhold.

Nessa's boom box was torn from her back and was swept away down the stairs with sickening cracks and crunches as it was dashed against the walls. Demelza wrapped her arms around the rail and clung on tight, her muscles screaming as the water threatened to carry Nessa away and take Demelza with her.

"Undo the rope!" shouted Nessa, gasping and spitting out water as she was tossed around like a rag doll.

"Never!" yelled Demelza, clinging on for dear life. Her fingers began to slip from the rail as Nessa's weight and the fast-flowing water began to drag her down. Just as the last of the strength was sapped from her arms, there was a cry of relief from Nessa. The rope around Demelza's waist suddenly loosened as Nessa finally caught hold of the rail and began dragging herself back up the stairs.

"Go-go-go!" she shouted.

Demelza didn't need telling twice. The ground floor was completely flooded now, and the water level was rising so rapidly that they were racing to stay ahead of it. Finally they reached the top and flung the tapestry aside as they charged into the corridor.

"Farewell, brave maidens!" Sir Cubert called as his transparent form flew from his tapestry. He sped alongside them for a moment, then disappeared through a wall.

The corridor was filling up fast as water came flooding through every one of the slit windows.

"The tower is above sea level," said Nessa. "We'll be okay once we reach it." Demelza nearly fell into the cascading water as the castle shook again. "As long as we haven't sunk too far!" Nessa added.

Demelza wasn't sure how they managed to stagger to the end of the corridor. Her whole body ached, and her lungs felt close to bursting, but she and Nessa dragged themselves through the archway at the bottom of the tower. Demelza sighed with relief as the stairs turned out to be dry, and they began to crawl up them, panting hard.

"Nearly there," gasped Nessa behind her as they climbed, legs like lead in their wet clothes. Demelza realized they must have climbed above sea level as the water wasn't rising behind them.

After what seemed like a year, they reached the trapdoor at the top of the tower. Putting their backs to it, they heaved with all their might until it lifted and crashed to the ground. Demelza clambered out onto the top of the tower, blinking hard against the morning sun.

"We did it. We got out!" she shouted to the whole world as Captain Honkers flew down into her open arms, honking with

delight to see her. He was shaking with fright over the noise and rumbling but had not abandoned his post.

"It's morning," said Nessa slowly. "It didn't seem like we were away that long. That curse must have made time pass in a funny way."

There was a rumble like an earthquake, and they stumbled as the castle began to rise from the sea, water rushing back out of every window. "We might be out," said Nessa. "Now we just need to get off this thing!"

Chapter Fifteen
NESSA'S SECRET

The whole world seemed to be shaking as the castle slowly rose from the sea. Nessa's bridge was fast becoming a ramp down to the cliff as it was lifted by the rising castle.

"The bikes!" shouted Demelza. Neon Justice was rattling toward the edge of the turret. Nessa lunged for it, but she was too late—as if in slow motion, the bike toppled down into the sea.

Demelza leapt to save her own bike from the same fate, then glanced at the bridge—it was only moments from dropping down onto the rocks. She leapt astride her bike and lined it up with the sloping bridge, yelling to Nessa, "Get on!"

Nessa leapfrogged onto the long seat behind Demelza and clung to her waist, whispering into her ear, "You can do it, D!"

Demelza rolled her front tire onto the ramp. The bike wobbled as the castle shook again.

If she was going to do it, it had to be now. She took a deep breath and pushed off. The ramp bounced and shook beneath them, so steep that Demelza didn't even have to pedal. She held on firmly to the handlebars, struggling to keep the bike straight as it whizzed down the ramp toward the cliff, pedals whirling so fast they were almost a blur. Captain Honkers soared above, honking at Demelza to go faster.

She could feel Nessa's grip on her waist tighten as the bridge began to tilt to the right. There was only one thing for it.

"Bunny hop!" she shouted to Nessa. She pushed down, then pulled up on her handlebars, taking the bike into a wheelie, then bounced on the back wheel, pulling up on the pedals with her feet.

Nessa pulled with her, and the whole bike soared up from the ramp just as it fell away, spinning down into the sea. Demelza's heart was in her mouth as they sailed through the air and came crashing down onto the cliff edge.

They leapt up immediately, scrabbling away from the edge, then dropped onto the grass with relief. Captain Honkers landed on Demelza's chest and buried his head in her hair, honking gently.

The castle continued to rise as they lay watching it from the cliff, legs still too shaky to stand. Soon the sea stack towers, which had always been level with the cliff, loomed high above them. Demelza crawled to the edge and looked down. The whole castle was now above water. Seaweed and barnacles clung to the stonework, and the occasional surprised fish wriggled out of the windows and flopped back down into the sea. The castle was standing on a huge outcrop of rock, which had risen with it.

"You know..." she said, as a realization suddenly hit. "If we'd just stayed on the tower, we could have walked downstairs and left through the front door once the water had flowed back out."

Nessa stared at her, then began to laugh. They laughed until tears streamed down their faces and their cheeks ached. When they finally managed to coax their legs into standing, Demelza cast a wistful look at the castle.

"I wish we'd been able to take just a tiny bit of that treasure. We're really going to have to move now." She looked over at the golf course and the camper park beyond it. "I've really loved living here. And so did Mom."

A strange expression had crept over Nessa's face. "So,

Demelza..." she said, staring at her feet. "I've, uh, got a confession to make. There was a reason I came to your camper park the other night. I wanted to—"

"Dad!" yelled Demelza, cutting Nessa off as her dad came striding toward them, his gaze fixed on the towering castle.

"Demelza, I thought you were still in bed," he said absent-mindedly as he stopped and stared up at the castle in awe, his hand resting on her shoulder.

"Look, Dad!" she said, waving up at the castle. "Me an' Nessa went inside and met the Penfurzy knights. We tried to bring some treasure back for you, but the cursed mist that ate Sir Warleggan wouldn't let us and made it all vanish."

Her dad stared at her for a minute without blinking. His mouth was hanging open, but any words seemed to be stuck somewhere in his throat. His eyes moved to Nessa, and he finally recovered the ability to speak.

"So, Nessa..." he began.

"Who's Nessa?" she replied. "I'm Cyndi, remember? Cyndi Lennox."

"Really? So you're not the daughter of Mr. and Mrs. Chakravarty who are staying in the hotel in town?"

"What? No," said Nessa, glaring at him accusingly. "Why do you assume I'm related to them?"

"Because Mr. Chakravarty told me he has a daughter called Nessa and showed me a picture of you in his wallet."

Demelza noticed Nessa's ears turning red.

"That could be anyone," said Nessa. "I bet she didn't even look like me."

"You were wearing the jacket you have on now. With the same patches. And those earrings. And that hairstyle. And..."

"Okay," said Nessa. "I know them. They're kidnappers. I've been on the run from them for years."

"He said the photo was taken last month. They were in it, too. You were all smiling."

"Fine." Nessa sighed. "You got me. That's my mom and dad."

Demelza's jaw hit the floor. "You're not an orphan?"

"I might as well be," said Nessa. "They abandoned me in a prison with a cruel warden."

"They told me they left you with your gran," said Demelza's dad. "I met them for breakfast in town this morning. They were pretty shocked to hear that you're here, too."

Demelza stared up at her dad. "Why were you having break-fast with Nessa's parents?"

Demelza's dad rubbed his chin. "Before I drive her down to them, I think we'd all better have a chat. Come on inside."

Captain Honkers hurried after them as they trooped into the kitchen. Demelza and Nessa sat silently at the table as Demelza's dad made cups of hot chocolate.

"So," he said, setting down the cups and a plate of biscuits that Captain Honkers immediately started pecking at. "There really was a Nessa who helped drive Bert's digger off the cliff."

"Told you!" said Demelza. She turned to Nessa. "So why are you really on Penfurzy, and why did you tell me fibs about your mom and dad?"

Nessa picked at one of her fingernails. "I wanted to see the island and the camper park for myself, seeing as they want to buy it and drag me here."

"WHAT?" said Demelza, unable to believe her ears. She leapt to her feet and slapped her hands down on the table, sending Captain Honkers flapping away from the biscuits in fright. "So you really are a spy? You came here to help your parents steal our home?"

"Demelza," said her dad in a warning tone. "Sit down, and use your indoor voice."

"It's not like that," said Nessa. "I was going to tell you. You know how you didn't want to move from here? Well, I didn't want to move from my home to live on a boring little island."

"Boring?" said Demelza. "Penfurzy's not boring! It's the best place there is!"

"I know that now," said Nessa. "At first I wanted to help you find the treasure so that your dad wouldn't sell to my parents. But then I had so much fun that I realized I wanted to stay here."

"So THAT'S why you wanted me to give back the treasure! You want my home for yourself." Demelza folded her arms across her chest and fought the urge to leap across the table at the girl who she had thought was her friend. She wasn't sure what she was angrier about—losing her home or Nessa's deceit.

"No. I want to be able to hang out with you any time I want, but I don't want you to have to leave," said Nessa. "It's the last thing I want. You have to believe me!"

"If I could get a word in?" said Nessa's dad. "No one is losing their home."

"I'm not moving to Penfurzy?" said Nessa, a mix of emotions passing over her face.

"You're not selling? We're not moving?" Demelza asked her dad, excitement bubbling in her stomach.

"We're staying right here, but Nessa is still moving to Penfurzy."

Demelza's brows knitted together as she tried to work out what her dad was saying.

"Nessa's parents are buying into the camper park and golf course. We're keeping our home, and they're buying that converted windmill just outside town."

Demelza's heart soared as she leapt to her feet and hugged her dad tightly. She turned to Nessa and noticed that she was beaming from ear to ear. Maybe she really hadn't wanted to take their home after all.

"I'll bet everyone will want to visit your camper site now, just to see the castle," said Nessa.

"Speaking of which, why is there an

ancient castle suddenly overlooking the golf course?" asked Demelza's dad.

"Oh, it's a GOOD story," said Demelza. "Get your listening ears ready, and I'll tell you all about our quest. But first I need to talk to Nessa, in private."

Chapter Sixteen
A BOX OF QUESTS

"So, if you're not an orphan, I guess you're not a spy, ninja, pirate, or rally driver, either?" said Demelza as she walked through the golf course with Nessa, Captain Honkers flapping around them, snapping at flies.

Nessa shook her head. "I'm sorry I didn't tell you everything, D. I came here to see how awful the place my parents wanted to buy was. I was really surprised when it wasn't awful at all. But, when I saw how much your home and the golf course meant to you, I wanted to help you save it, even if it meant we wouldn't be moving here."

"You really do care, then?" asked Demelza.

"Of course I care. Spit sisters, remember?" Nessa held out her hand.

Demelza looked at it for a moment, then grasped it tightly. "Spit sisters," she said. "Forever."

"I guess you'll have to update the golf course now," said Nessa as they reached the last hole. "You know, with our bits— the breaking of the curse and the raising of the castle."

"Ooh, great idea!" said Demelza. She rubbed her nose. "You can help if you want?"

"I'd like that," said Nessa. "You don't think, maybe, we could look for another adventure, too?"

"The best adventures find you," said Demelza. "That's what Mom always said. But, before we go adventuring again, you need a new steed."

"Don't worry, I'll be bringing my own bike over when we move here," said Nessa. "Did I tell you I won it from Evel Knievel when he dared me to leap through three flaming hoops? Ow!" She rubbed her arm where Demelza had punched it. "Okay," she admitted as Demelza glared at her. "I lied again. It was only two hoops."

"Is everything you say a big fib?" Demelza asked as they passed hole five, which featured the Penfurzy knights carrying chests full of gold on their backs.

"No," said Nessa. "I'm genuinely sorry you didn't get to keep any treasure."

"Well, we kinda did find treasure in the end," said Demelza.

"Huh? What treasure?"

"The best treasure of all," said Demelza. "One that can't fade away or get used up. You know, the special treasure we found aboard our ship?"

"I have no idea what you're talking about right now," said Nessa.

Demelza beamed up at her. "Our frieeeendship!" she sang.

"That," said Nessa looking down at her and shaking her head, "has to be the cheesiest thing I have ever heard."

"Then it's a good job you're sticking around," said Demelza, "'cause there's PLENTY more where that came from!"

Nessa laughed, and the two of them linked arms as they made their way back to the house, Captain Honkers pattering happily along behind them.

That night, Demelza stayed in the main house for the first

time in months. Nessa was staying with her parents in the hotel in town. Demelza and her dad were sitting in armchairs in front of the fire, and Captain Honkers was snoozing on the back of Demelza's chair, his head hanging down so that his chin rested on her shoulder. She had shown her dad the notebook that had guided them on their quest, and they were now looking through family photo albums and talking about her mom.

"She'd be proud of you, you know," said her dad, turning the notebook over in his hands.

"I know," said Demelza. "I'm happy we found the castle for her. I just wish the adventure wasn't over."

"Maybe it doesn't have to be," said her dad, slapping the arm of his chair and jumping up as if he'd just remembered something. "I'll be right back!"

Demelza wondered what he was doing as she watched him manhandle a ladder upstairs. Honkers woke up and raised his head from her shoulder as she listened to her dad thumping and bumping around in the attic, searching for something. She looked down at the photo she was holding of her mom and dad swinging her by the arms.

"We found it for you, Mom," she said, stroking the photo.

"We found the treasure you were looking for and ended the curse, once and for all."

"Got it!" shouted her dad, hurrying back downstairs with a cardboard box. He blew the dust from the lid then plonked it onto Demelza's knee. "Here you go. Open it."

She peeled the sellotape off it, opened the flaps and peered inside. "Notebooks?" she said, looking up at her dad.

"Your mom's notebooks." He sat down next to her. "She'd want you to have them."

Demelza reached into the box and pulled out one with a green leather cover that read, "The Penfurzy Pendragon Puzzle." Another bore the words "The Legend of the Golden Hare," the next "The Piskies of Penfurzy." Each notebook was filled with little sketches and notes on Penfurzy's most intriguing mysteries and legends. Demelza felt a tingle of excitement starting in her scalp and fizzing all the way down to her toes.

"Your mother's quests," said her dad. "I reckon she'd love you to continue them."

Demelza flung her arms around him. The thought of countless new adventures made her feel as though she was floating toward the ceiling.

"On behalf of myself and Nessa, I accept these quests," she said in her gravest of voices, hand over her heart. "Not for riches, not for glory, but for Mom. May we quest forever in her name!"

END

(FOR NOW)

Acknowledgments

When you're approached to write a book just after you have a newborn baby, I believe the correct response is to run screaming in the opposite direction; however, there are some projects that can't be turned down, especially ones with people who are a joy to collaborate with. Knights Of are a wonderful publisher on a noble quest to bring more diversity to publishing and to make books better. I am very grateful to them, especially Aimée and David, for inviting me to be their very first author.

I am very excited that Knights and Bikes is cycling all the way across the Atlantic and want to thank my U.S. editor, Molly, and the rest of the Sourcebooks team for sharing Nessa and Demelza's adventures with a new audience.

As someone who spent the eighties playing video games, recording mixtapes, collecting bread tags for my bike, and searching for adventure with my best friend, I was overjoyed to be asked to write about two funny, gross, adventurous girls living my childhood, especially as it was based on a game I was already backing on Kickstarter. Rex's illustrations of Nessa, Demelza, and Captain Honkers were so full of joy and energy that they leapt off the screen and pretty much wrote themselves. Thanks for trusting me with your world, Rex and Moo.

Luke Newell did a wonderful job of bringing this book to life with hilarious illustrations. I love to see his interpretation of my words as he always adds something new to them. Marssaié quite literally takes my words and makes them look awesome with her brilliant design skills.

Squeezy hugs are due to my husband, Satish, for his support and for being my first reader. He would like me to make you all aware that the Prince joke was his suggestion.

Finally, but most importantly, this book could never have been finished if it wasn't for my parents helping me out A LOT, from helping with childcare to housework, cooking, and stopping me procrastinating.

Thank you, Mom and Dad.

About the Author

Gabrielle lives in the northeast of England with her husband, daughter, and rather silly cat. She loves books and video games. She plays video games, makes video games, and even taught students to design video games, so she was very excited to get to write a book based on a brilliant video game: this very book you are holding! As well as three Knights and Bikes books, Gabrielle is also the author of the Alfie Bloom series.

ME AND NESSA HOPE YOU ENJOYED OUR ADVENTURE WHAT GABRIELLE WROTE DOWN IN THIS BOOK!

BUT THERES A WHOLE OTHER STORY (THAT YOU CAN PLAY!) IN THE KNIGHTS AND BIKES VIDEO-GAME!!

YOU CAN FEED CAPTAIN HONKER

YOU CAN RIDE AROUND ON BIKES!

SCARE AWAY THE BADDIES

WWW.FOAMSWORDGAMES.COM

KNIGHTS AND BIKES

REBEL BICYCLE CLUB

COMING SOON!